Goodie

Veronica Heley

John Hunt
Publishing Limited

Copyright © 2002 John Hunt Publishing Ltd Text © 2002 Veronica Heley
Reissued by John Hunt Publishing Ltd. 2002.

Cover illustration by Alice Englander

ISBN 1 84298 075 0

Typography by Graham Whiteman Design

Write to: John Hunt Publishing Ltd
46A West Street, Alresford, Hampshire SO24 9AU UK

The rights of Veronica Heley as author of this work have been asserted in
accordance with the Copyright, Designs and Patents Act 1988.

A CIP catalogue record for this book is available from the British Library.

Printed in Great Britain by Ashford Colour Press.

Visit us on the Web at: www.johnhunt-publishing.com

1

'I wish I could have stayed at home with you, Daddy,' said Kate. 'I'd have been ever so good.' Her voice wobbled, though she was trying not to cry.

'We've been over this, Poppet. I can't leave you in the house alone and all your friends have gone away for half-term.'

'But you're taking me so far away. Suppose something happens to Mummy…'

'Nothing's going to happen to your mother,' said Kate's daddy. He sounded as if he meant it. 'The doctors are very clever. They'll soon find out what's making your mother ill and make her well again in next to no time.'

Kate hoped he was right, but she couldn't get out of her mind the awful way her mummy had looked when she had suddenly doubled over in pain. Kate had never felt so scared in all her life as when her mummy was taken off in the ambulance. Now she was being driven to another town to stay with people she didn't know, and it was all too much for her.

She said, 'Couldn't I have stayed with someone I know? I can't remember Aunty Pat, or my cousin Claire.'

'You did meet them when you were small. They've only just moved back down from the North, or I'd have taken you over to see them before this.'

Kate sniffed and felt for a tissue to blow her nose. The car stopped at some traffic lights and Daddy put his arm around her to give her a hug.

'Now, Poppet, I know this is all very difficult for you, but I promise I will ring you every evening to let you know how Mummy's getting on. And if they keep her in hospital for more than a couple of days, I'll try to get over to see you one afternoon.'

Kate nodded but felt for her hanky.

Daddy said, 'That's my brave girl.'

Kate sniffed. It was all very well for her daddy. He was really and truly a hero. He'd rescued a boy from a burning house and got a medal for it. Kate knew she was no heroine. She couldn't help it. She'd been born afraid.

'I think this is it,' said Daddy, driving up a hill and turning into a cul-de-sac called Pine Tree Close.

Five modern detached houses were arranged around a circular turning space. Five pine trees leaned over the roofs of the houses. The wind shivered their shaggy tops and whispered '…strangers…we don't like s-strangers…'

Kate's daddy took her bag out of the car and dumped it on the pavement, along with Nibbles in his cat basket.

A very thin, dark-haired woman with a no-nonsense face came out of one of the houses and said, 'So there you are at last, Don! Have you time for a cuppa?'

'I'll get straight back to the hospital if you don't mind, Pat,' said Kate's daddy, giving his sister an absent-minded sort of kiss. 'I'm sorry to lumber you with Kate at such short notice, but I was at my wits' end what to do.'

'Think nothing of it,' said Aunty Pat. 'I'm out all day at work, but I'm sure the girls will play happily together. Anyway, I've got an au pair.'

A plump girl with spiky black hair came out of the house and stared at Kate. She had glittery make-up around her eyes which made her look like a bad-tempered doll. She was ultra-fashionable in a white T-shirt with more glitter on it, white jeans and high-heeled boots. Claire was almost eleven - the same age as Kate - but she looked far older.

Kate was the very opposite of Claire. Kate had long fair hair as straight as could be, drifting around her shoulders. Her mummy had never let her wear make-up except for play, because she said it would spoil Kate's lovely skin. Kate was wearing her velvety blue track suit and matching trainers. She'd been quite happy with her appearance until she saw Claire looking down her nose at her.

'What's that?' said Claire, aiming a kick at the cat basket.

'That's Nibbles,' said Kate, rescuing the basket. 'My kitten. He's too new to be left behind in an empty house.'

3

'I suppose he'll make messes everywhere,' said Claire. 'Well, don't expect me to clear up after him!' She meant it, too. She gave Kate a filthy look.

Kate realised that Claire didn't want her to stay, any more than Kate had wanted to come. Kate took hold of her father's coat and drew him a little way round the car, so the others couldn't hear.

She said, 'Don't leave me here, Daddy.'

'I'm sorry, Poppet, but I must. You'll be all right. Don't cry, now. Here, catch a hold of this bag. There's a couple of new books in it for you. Hope you like them. Give us a kiss, now.'

He kissed her, got into his car and drove off down the hill.

Aunty Pat and Claire looked at Kate as if they didn't know what to do next.

'Please,' said Kate, 'could I let Nibbles out and feed him? I've got his tins and biscuits in my bag.'

Claire rolled her eyes and walked back into the house. Aunty Pat looked cross but led the way through the house and into a large bright kitchen at the back. Standing by the stove was a tall, fair-haired girl who looked too fragile for the heavy stew-pan she was lifting into the oven.

'Eloise,' said Aunty Pat. 'This is Kate, whom I told you about. Kate, this is Eloise, our au pair. She'll look after you and your cat.'

The phone rang and Aunty Pat went to answer it. Kate felt dreadful. Not only had Claire ignored her, but Aunty Pat hadn't made her feel welcome, either.

Eloise held out her hands to Kate and smiled.

4

'Kate is a nice name, yes? I have a little sister called Caterina, which is the same, I think. I come from Switzerland. Do you know where is Switzerland? It is a long way away. But now I live 'ere and I 'elp your aunt around the house. Your cat, what is she called?'

'It's a he, and he's called Nibbles.'

Kate liked Eloise and she could feel that Eloise liked her. Together they let Nibbles out for a run in the back garden and found some unbreakable dishes for his milk and biscuits. Then Nibbles gave himself a thorough wash while Kate helped Eloise with the supper. Eloise said the family usually ate in the kitchen although there was a dining-room for special occasions.

Eloise spoke in a funny accent, but if she made a mistake in her English Kate smiled and then Eloise smiled, too. They were getting on fine when Claire came in, sat down and demanded her supper in what Kate thought was a very rude manner.

'It is coming, Claire,' said Eloise, 'One minute, two per'aps.'

'You forgot your 'h' again,' said Claire, scornfully.

Kate opened her eyes wide. In her home, anyone who spoke so rudely to a grown-up, especially someone from another country, would have been told off for it. Eloise blushed but said nothing as she put the food on the table.

Aunty Pat joined them for supper but she was too busy with some paperwork to talk to them. She explained to Kate that it might be half-term for schoolchildren, but that she herself had to work all through and wouldn't have much time to give to them.

Kate made herself small, knowing without being told that Aunty Pat thought it was a great nuisance, having another child wished on her.

After supper Eloise took Kate upstairs and showed her where she was to sleep. She had a pretty room built over the garage at the side of the house. The curtains were patterned with blue and white and matched the duvet on the bed under the window. Also, which made Kate feel very important, there was a wash-hand basin of her very own in one corner of the room.

Claire came in to watch while Eloise and Kate unpacked Kate's bag.

'What's that?' said Claire, pointing to the bag of books her father had given her at the last minute.

'Some books my daddy picked out for me.' Claire didn't wait to be shown them, but upended the bag on Kate's bed. Two favourites, the latest Anne Fine's children's book and a hardback of the last Harry Potter.

Claire picked them up as if they smelt bad. 'Oh yuck. Do you have to read all this while you're here?'

Eloise said to Kate. 'Claire does not read books. She plays computer games instead.'

'That's nice,' said Kate. 'I haven't got a computer, though my daddy has.'

'I thought everyone had computers nowadays. All my friends have them.'

Most of Kate's friends did, too, but she hated to agree with Claire about anything, so she didn't reply.

Claire seemed to think she had scored a point over Kate, so she continued, 'My mother says that your father is whiter than perfect. What do you think she means by that?'

Kate understood that Claire meant to be rude. She coloured up and said, 'Well, he did save that boy from the house that was on fire. Do you mean that?'

Claire pulled face. 'I suppose he's all holy and Chrissy and goes to church all the time!'

'No,' said Kate, puzzled. 'We don't go to church, except Christmas and stuff.'

When Eloise had bent over, Kate had spotted a gold cross on a chain around her neck. Was Eloise a Christian? She might be. Eloise had been kind to her. So Kate wondered if Claire were also being rude to Eloise as well.

'Time for bed,' said Eloise. Kate suddenly realised how tired she felt. Claire left to get undressed while Kate washed and used the lovely soft towel Eloise had found for her. Eloise said goodnight, while Kate climbed up into her bed by the window and reached for her Harry Potter.

Before she could open it, in came Aunty Pat, followed by Claire. 'Now children,' said Aunty Pat, looking at her watch. 'I've got to go out to a meeting, but I've just time to tell you a story before I go.'

'Tell the one about the ghost,' said Claire, sitting on Kate's bed.

7

Kate was just going to say that she didn't particularly want to hear stories about ghosts, when Aunty Pat started.

'Once upon a time,' said Aunty Pat, 'all the land around here belonged to the old house on top of the hill. Kate, if you look out of the window up the hill, you'll be able to see it.'

Kate looked out of the window. Darkness had crept around them some time ago, but there was a moon and a street light shone somewhere nearby. Through the shifting branches of the pine trees, Kate caught sight of a winking light far up the hill to the right.

'I can see a light,' said Kate.

'That's from the top of the house. A beautiful girl called Belle lived up there with her rich parents and many, many men wanted to marry her. Down here where our house now stands, there were just two tumbledown old cottages where some of the outdoor servants lived, gardeners and the like. The son of one of the gardeners was called Tomkin and he worked up at the big house as a groom. He helped to look after the horses and sometimes he brought them down here to drink in a pond that used to be in front of our house.'

'…and he was in love with Belle,' said Claire.

'Yes, but that was a secret, because if anyone had found out, he'd have been laughed at by all the other servants.'

'If I'd been Belle,' said Claire, 'I'd have run away with Tomkin.'

'Perhaps you would and perhaps you wouldn't,' said Aunty Pat. 'In those days daughters were whipped if they disobeyed their parents and sent to bed without any supper. Very probably Belle never knew that Tomkin was in love with her, even though he used to creep up to the big house every evening, to see if he could catch sight of her moving around the house in one of her beautiful evening gowns.

'One day Belle was driven down the hill to be married to a rich friend of her father's. Tomkin stood on the back of the carriage in the groom's place to take her to church and that night he slipped away and was never seen again. Some people say that he ran away to sea, but others say he drowned himself in the pond outside. The story goes that sometimes, on dark nights, you can still see his ghost climbing the path to the big house, to catch a glimpse of his long-lost love.'

Kate felt a lump come into her throat to think of poor Tomkin, but Claire was bouncing around on the bed in excitement. 'If I'd been Tomkin,' she said, 'I'd have blown them all up and run off with Belle.'

'He was only a poor gardener's boy,' said Aunty Pat, laughing. 'Now, Kate, no need to look so tragic. There's no such thing as a ghost, you know.'

'I bet there is,' said Claire, pressing her nose to the window. 'I bet he still walks up this path every night, only there's no one here to see, because no one sleeps in this room usually.'

'You mean, this very path outside my window?' said Kate, in a quavering voice.

'Scaredy cat!' said Claire. 'I thought you'd be scared!'

'Now children, don't quarrel,' said her mother in a sharp voice. 'Off to bed with you, lights out, and No More Noise!'

Claire flounced out after her mother leaving Kate alone in the dark. She heard Aunty Pat take the car out of the garage and drive off down the hill.

Aunty Pat had turned off the light when she left and Kate was too scared to get out of bed to turn it on again. Suppose something grabbed at her ankles between the bed and the door!

Suppose the ghost came into the house from outside! But of course there weren't any such things as ghosts, not really.

Aunty Pat had forgotten to draw the curtains across the window. Kate told herself to sit up and draw them. If she could do that, she might be brave enough to get out of bed and cross the room to the light switch.

There was a street light on the corner of the path a little way up the hill, but it didn't help much. The alleyway was all dark and mysterious. Kate could imagine all sorts of terrible things going on down there in the dark. Perhaps a man was hiding in the shadows, waiting to leap out on you. It would be a good place for a mugger to hide, even though there didn't seem to be anybody going up and down the alley at this time of the evening.

The shadows were so dense under the hedge, that you couldn't make out what was hedge and what was path. Clouds passed across the moon, and the trees shifted and shivered. The shape of the shadow under the hedge altered and split into two. One part of the shadow broke away and crept up the path. It was moving like a spider, bending low, black all over…

Kate screamed and dived under the duvet.

Kate wanted her daddy and her mummy. Especially her mummy. She remembered that her mummy was in hospital. Kate had forgotten all about her mummy being in hospital for a little while, what with everything being so different at Aunty Pat's. But now she began to worry about her mummy. Daddy had promised to ring and let Kate know what was going on, but he hadn't done so. Perhaps he'd meant he'd only ring tomorrow.

Kate cried a little, quietly. She missed Nibbles, who usually went to sleep curled up on her pillow. Aunty Pat had said she didn't allow cats upstairs in her house.

Kate was so unhappy she didn't know what to do with herself.

She was still too frightened to get out of bed.

Her eyes were growing accustomed to the dark.

Kate wanted Nibbles! It was awful without him. She hoped he was all right downstairs. Probably he was missing her as much as she was missing him. And her mummy. And her daddy.

She heard Eloise speaking on the phone downstairs. There was a crack of light showing under the door. Kate thought that if she were very brave, perhaps she could get out of bed and rush over to the door and open it, just a bit. She was sure she would sleep better if she could see a light on in the passage. At that very moment the door opened and Claire marched in, putting on the light as she did so.

'I keep my stash of sweets in your cupboard so's nobody can find them,' she said. 'I forgot to take them out when I heard you were coming.' She opened the cupboard door and took out a bag of sweets. She put one in her mouth and started crunching but didn't offer any to Kate. 'Were you asleep?'

'No,' said Kate. 'I was frightened. I thought I saw something move on the path below - something strange.'

Claire burst out laughing. 'I bet you thought it was the ghost! You did! You really thought you'd seen the ghost, didn't you?'

'I did see something,' said Kate. 'I wasn't imagining it!'

Eloise came into the room, smiling, but shaking her head at them. 'I hear you, playing when you should be in bed. Claire, you should not eat sweets at night. Go to brush your teeth. Kate, that was your father on the phone. Your mother is a little better and he will ring you again tomorrow.'

Claire said, 'Kate's stupid! She thought she saw Tomkin's ghost!'

Eloise bent over to kiss Kate. 'Goodnight, Kate. No more dreams, no?'

'It wasn't a dream,' said Kate, snuggling down. Or was it? Had she imagined it, really? She really did feel tired. She had had a long day, full of happenings. Eloise pushed Claire out of the room, but left the door ajar. Kate thought she liked Eloise a lot, and then she fell asleep.

2

Pine Tree Close looked different in the daytime. The pine trees had shrunk back to ordinary size, and were not talking to themselves any more.

Kate looked up the alley at the side of the house. On the right was Aunty Pat's house and garden, bounded by an old stone wall. But on the other side of the alley there was a high privet hedge. Half way up the hill the path bent round to the right and on this corner stood a lamp post.Kate felt shivery all over again, looking up that path. Even in the daytime, it was a dark and dreary place.

She tried to imagine the Close as it had been long ago with the tumbledown cottages and the pond in the middle of the road. There wouldn't have been any tarmac. The ground would have been dusty in summer and slippery with ice and snow in the winter. Perhaps the gardener had kept hens and ducks which would have swum in the pond. She'd seen pictures of cottages like that.

Claire came out of the house and pointed up the hill. 'That's the house where Belle lived. Her great-

great - I don't know how many greats - granddaughter lives there now, all alone. But she isn't beautiful or even rich any more. I know all about it because I visit her every week to take her some eggs and some of Mummy's magazines. The people who lived here before used to take her eggs and they asked us to carry on visiting her, so I do. I wouldn't bother, but it's an easy way to get my Service badge for Guides. Are you in the Guides? How many badges have you got? I've got eight so far.'

Kate had nine but didn't like to say so because it would sound like boasting. Instead she said, 'Do you go up there all by yourself? You're very brave.'

'Yes, of course. I'm not scared. Sometimes my friend Tracy comes and sometimes Eloise does, but usually I go by myself. Mummy's too busy. You can come with me this week if Tracy can't make it.'

Aunty Pat had already gone off to work in her office, so after Kate had helped clear up in the kitchen, Eloise took them down the hill into the town centre. They bought a get well card for Kate's mummy and sent it off. Then they went to the swimming baths.

Kate wasn't a brilliant swimmer but she could manage a width of the baths if she wasn't hurried. Claire had been to the baths almost every day in the summer holidays. Not only could she swim two lengths without stopping, but she could also swim under water.

Kate tried to explain that she could only swim a bit but Claire was impatient.

'Oh, come on, Kate! Let's have some fun!'

Claire plunged under water and snatched at Kate's legs.

Kate screamed and splashed to the side.

'Really, Claire!' said Eloise. 'You must more careful be!'

Claire screeched with laughter. '"More careful be!" You are silly, Eloise. You can't even speak English properly!'

Eloise went red but persisted. 'You will make an accident!'

'Oh, rotten Eloise, shut up!' Claire went off to practise diving off the lower of the two boards.

'I'm s-sorry,' said Kate to Eloise. 'I didn't mean to make a fuss.'

'Is all right. Now we try again, no? Softly, a little way at a time...'

Kate began to enjoy herself. Eloise was so patient that Kate grew more confident and began to think she might manage a whole length of the baths, with luck! Then, when Eloise was helping another child to climb out of the water, Claire danced up and dragged Kate off to the high diving board.

'Come and watch me!' cried Claire. 'I'm just ace at diving!'

'It's awfully high,' said Kate, climbing slowly after Claire. 'I wish I could dive, but it scares me to look down.'

'Scaredy cat!' cried Claire. 'It's easy peasy, watch me!' Claire tumbled forward off the board and dived in, all anyhow.

A couple of large boys brushed past Kate and dived in, neatly. Claire climbed the steps again, grinning. 'Did you see that? Aren't I good?'

'Yes,' said Kate. 'I think I'll climb back down now.'

'Don't be silly! You've got to dive in!'

'I can't!'

'Jump, or I'll push you!'

'No, you...'

Claire rushed at Kate with outstretched arms. Kate tried to step back, but there was nothing there for her to tread on...and even as she clutched at Claire to save herself, she fell...backwards, with a scream...

As she fell she saw Claire laughing and falling on top of her.

They went down into the water together. Kate could feel the water closing in around her and she panicked. She was never going to get out of that pool alive She was going to drown...

Then she was lying face down on a hard surface. Choking and coughing.

'Up you come, no harm done,' said a man's voice above her.

Kate coughed up some more water and then was able to sit up in Eloise's arms. Someone had brought a towel and Eloise wrapped it around her. Kate was shivering. She tried to stop but didn't seem able to do so. There was a horrid raw feeling at the back of her nose and throat which made it hard to speak.

'All right now?' said the man. He was one of the

17

pool attendants and looked strong enough to drag a dozen children at a time out of the pool.

'Yes,' said Kate. Or that's what she tried to say, but it didn't come out properly, so she just nodded.

'As for you, my girl,' said the attendant to Claire. 'You're lucky you didn't kill your friend, behaving in such a dangerous way.'

'It was an accident,' said Claire, trying to shrug it off. 'How was I to know she'd be so stupid? If she couldn't dive, she shouldn't have gone up onto the high board.'

Kate felt tears come to her eyes. How could Claire lie like that! Kate felt too tired to argue, so she let Eloise lead her away to the changing room. Eloise got her a hot milky drink and that helped, but walking home seemed to take a long time.

Claire was having lunch with her friend Tracy, so Eloise had time to spend with Kate. Kate felt pretty awful even after she got home, so Eloise tucked her up in a big chair and put Nibbles on her lap.

Kate tried to face the fact that Claire really didn't like her. It wasn't easy. It was bad enough for Kate to be so worried about her mummy, and having to stay away from home. She had a dull, empty feeling in her middle, whenever she thought about her mummy, Of course that horrid feeling would have been just the same if she'd been at home, but it was far worse because of having to stay with people who didn't like her.

Eloise brought Kate a mug of hot milk and coaxed her to drink it.

'Thank you, Eloise,' said Kate.

Eloise sat down beside her and stroked Kate's hands.

'Now, Kate. You sleep for a little, yes?'

Eloise was so kind that it made Kate want to cry. She hadn't meant to say anything about Claire, but it just burst out of her. 'Why doesn't Claire like me?'

'She does, per'aps. It is just that she is - how you say - in a bad patch.'

'Going through a bad patch?'

'Yes. She loves 'er father very much, but 'e goes away on business for a long time, yes, a very long time. Claire's mother does not speak of 'im, never. Not to me, not to Claire. I think per'aps poor Claire thinks she will never see 'im again.'

Kate had a friend at school whose father had walked out one day and never come back, and three more whose parents were divorced.

'They are going to be divorced?'

Eloise raised her shoulders to her ears and let them drop. 'No one knows. Per'aps, per'aps not. Claire is angry all the time, because of this bad situation. You go to church sometimes, Kate, so you understand about being kind to people who are feeling hurt, no? We must try to forgive Claire and to love 'er, and to pray for 'er.'

Kate could hardly believe her ears. She wasn't going to try to love Claire! No way! Not after Claire had been so awful to her! As for praying for her...what a daft idea! Even if she knew how, which she didn't. Or even believe in it.

'Is hard, no?' said Eloise, smiling.

'Too hard,' said Kate, not smiling back.

'Is necessary,' said Eloise, becoming serious. 'Claire's mummy is busy all the time, making money to pay the bills. Someone must love Claire and 'elp her. I think per'aps God sent you 'ere to 'elp Claire.'

'God wouldn't make my mummy ill!'

'No, no. But while you are 'ere, it is a special job for you, no?'

'No,' said Kate firmly. 'I really am not Claire's sort. She thinks I'm a scaredy cat, and I expect she's right. But she needn't go on about it.'

'I'm scared, too.'

Kate stared. 'But you're grown up. Grown-ups aren't frightened of anything.'

'Yes, they are, sometimes. I am frightened of so many things when I come to this country. People laugh for the way I speak. In the shops the money it is different, and the food it is different, and I cry so much I think I will give up and go 'ome. But then I see that little Claire is needing me, so I stay. Every day I pray for 'er, and try to love 'er more.'

Kate was silent. She had never met anyone like Eloise before. She wanted Eloise to go on liking her, but perhaps that ought not to be under false pretences. 'You thought I was a Christian, but I don't think I am. I mean, we only go to church when it's carols and nativity plays and stuff like that. This prayer thing. Is that like asking for something you need?'

Eloise blushed and struck her forehead with her hand. 'Silly me! I made a jump in my mind. Sorry.

But you are a good person, you want to know about Jesus, no?'

'Tell me. We learned a bit at school, but it all seemed, well, just another lesson.'

'You know that God made the world and everything, with all the peoples. Then he said to the peoples, I don't want you to love me because you have to, but because you want to. Some did, and some didn't. Now and then God sent a man or a woman to remind everyone about him, and at the last he sent his son - that's Jesus. 'Jesus died and went back to Heaven, but he's still with us in a different way. If we love him and want him in our lives, he listens when we talk to him, comforts us when things are bad. We listen very hard, he tells us what to do.'

'That's a big thing.'

'A very big thing. I talk to Jesus every day. I tell him what is worrying, and thank him for what is good.'

'That is what you mean by praying? Will you pray for me, too? And for my mummy? I am so worried about her, Eloise. She was in such pain that I thought she'd die.'

Kate put both hands over her mouth, because she'd said the awful word 'die'. Her mummy wasn't going to die. No.

Eloise gave Kate a hug. 'I pray and you pray, and everything will be all right. Now we will 'ave a little something to eat and then per'aps you will have a rest. Then we will do some cooking, yes?'

'Yes, please,' said Kate.

That afternoon it rained, but Kate had such a good time helping Eloise with her baking, that she almost forgot about her mummy. Nibbles joined in the fun. His favourite game was leaping up at you when you were carrying things from the table to the fridge or the sink.

Eloise showed Kate how to make a ball out of crumpled paper and elastic bands for Nibbles to play with. They hung it from a knob on a cupboard, so that it swung this way and that when Nibbles patted it. Sometimes the ball swung right round and nudged Nibbles on the back of his head and then he went bananas, trying to fight it.

Eventually he tired himself out and went to sleep curled up on one of Eloise's sweaters in a corner.

Tracy's mummy brought Claire home just as Aunty Pat got back from the office and they all sat down to supper together. Claire had so much to say about what she'd been doing that afternoon, that the incident at the swimming pool was not mentioned. Kate was glad in a way, because she was trying not to think about it. She was still feeling tired and every now and then it came over her how nearly she'd drowned. She thought she'd never dare to go swimming again - at least, not with Claire around!

As for forgiving Claire or loving her - not likely!

Aunty Pat told them a different story at bedtime, about a brother and sister who dressed up in their parents' clothes and joined in a grown-up party when they were supposed to be safely tucked up in bed. Kate laughed and laughed, especially when Aunty Pat revealed that it was a true story, from the time when she and Kate's daddy had been children.

Kate was so tired that she only read for a short time when she got into bed, and only thought about talking to Jesus as she snuggled down under the duvet. She was too tired to think about it properly, but she did ask Him to look after her mummy. She didn't ask him to look after Claire, though. Not after what had happened.

Although she was so tired, when she closed her eyes she found she couldn't sleep for worrying about her mummy. Her daddy hadn't rung. Did that mean he'd forgotten all about her, as Claire's father seemed to have forgotten about her? Or did it mean that something dreadful had happened to Mummy?

Aunty Pat put her head round the door and said, 'Not asleep yet, Kate? You forgot to close your bedroom door.'

'Could you leave it open just a crack, please? Aunty Pat, you haven't heard from Daddy, have you?'

'No, dear, but I'm sure everything will be all right.'

'Could I have Nibbles to sleep with me? He sleeps with me at home.'

'You know I don't allow animals upstairs.'

Aunty Pat went out, closing the door behind her. Kate stuck it out for five minutes, then gritted her teeth and got up to open the door again. She really didn't like being in the dark in a strange place. If she let her thoughts wander, she'd start worrying about her mummy dying and about the water closing over her at the swimming baths. Then she'd think about the shadow down below in the alley, who might be looking up at her window at that very minute.

It was a windy night and the pine trees were rustling like mad. Kate was not used to pine trees. They were tall and thin all the way up, with heavy heads on top. Maybe, thought Kate, on such a windy night, one of the heads might snap off and come crashing down on her.

She did not sleep well and when she went down to breakfast, still feeling rather tired, she walked into trouble.

'That filthy cat!' cried Claire. 'He's made a mess right by the back door!'

'The poor thing!' said Eloise. 'Do not kick 'im, Claire. 'E must have tried to get out before we came down!'

'We have a cat-flap for him at home,' said Kate. 'And of course since he sleeps in my room, I know when to let him out.'

Claire aimed another kick at Nibbles, who thought she was playing and danced around her with pricked-up ears. Claire said, 'I'm not going to clear it up, and you needn't think I am.'

'It's Kate's cat and she will have to do it,' said Aunty Pat, who was trying to read some letters and eat her breakfast at the same time. 'Now I must rush, I've got a lot on today. Claire, don't forget the magazines for Miss Maine. There's a whole pile on the hall table, because you forgot to take any last week.'

'They're heavy,' grumbled Claire. 'Do I have to?'

'I expect Kate will help you, if you ask her,' said Aunty Pat. She picked up her coat, laptop and briefcase, and disappeared.

Claire stared at Kate, and Kate stared back.

'I suppose you can come with me, if you like,' said Claire. 'It'll be something to do. Tracy's busy this morning.'

Kate felt like saying something rude like, 'If you think I'm going to help you, after what you've done to me...' But she didn't, because Eloise was nodding and smiling across the table from them. Kate wanted to please Eloise, so she said she didn't mind helping Claire with the magazines.

'There's some fresh eggs to take, too,' said Claire. 'Mummy gets them from a farm. I'll carry the eggs and you can take the magazines.'

Kate was going to say that that wasn't fair because the magazines were heavy, but Eloise found her a basket on wheels for the magazines and it was good fun dragging that along.

The two children went up the alley at the side of the house. When they got round the corner where the lamp post stood, the path turned into steps climbing a steep bit of the hill. The steps had been made by setting split lengths of tree trunk sideways to hold back the earth. Kate found it was hard pulling the basket on wheels up the steps, especially since Claire refused to help her. A little way up the hill they came to a tall green door set in the high wall that bounded the garden of the big house.

'This is the quick way in,' said Claire. She tried the latch, but the door refused to budge.

Kate thought it was like a door in one of her story books. Who knew what might lie behind it? Perhaps a beautiful garden, with tinkling fountains and masses of roses, all blooming out of season. Perhaps there would be acres of flat green lawn, with peacocks parading around. It was exciting, wondering what might lie behind that sort of door.

Claire kicked the door in a temper, but it still wouldn't budge. Suddenly a dog started barking on the other side of the door. Kate jumped a mile and almost let go the handle of the basket on wheels. It sounded to her like a very large, very fierce guard dog.

'Oh dear,' said Kate. 'Does Miss Maine have a dog?'

'Yes, she does, and if you're not careful I'll set Fury on to you and he'll eat you up, so there!'

That made Kate feel worse than ever. She told herself that even a very large, very fierce dog couldn't really eat her up, but she did wish Eloise had come with them. If Eloise were there, the dog couldn't hurt her, could he?

They went on up the steps till they came to another green door. Here the walls were even higher.

'This is the door onto the terrace,' said Claire. 'If the garden gate is bolted on the inside, then Miss Maine usually leaves this door open for me.'

This door wouldn't budge, either. Now the dog started to bark again, much closer. He must have followed them up the garden, on his side of the wall.

'Oh, shut up, Fury!' shouted Claire.

Kate looked up and up. They were right under the house now. It loomed above them. There were little turrets on unexpected corners and right on top there was something that looked like a glassed-in verandah. Claire said it was called a lantern, and that it gave a light to the main staircase, but Kate knew better. Set high on the top of the hill like that, it was a light to guide the owners home on dark nights. Perhaps that was the light she could see from her bedroom window below. Kate thought the house looked like one of the castles in a Walt Disney film.

All the windows on the ground floor were shuttered, which gave the house a sleeping look.

The children went on and up following the wall till they came to a narrow lane which snaked off into the distance. On their right was a semi-circular driveway serving the big house, heavily overgrown with shrubs. Claire said that the lane led out into the country on one side, and on the other it went down the other side of the hill and through a housing estate before it got to the main road. That was why her mother made her come up the pathway to deliver the eggs and magazines. It was a long way round by car.

Claire led the way up some crumbling stone steps under a stone-pillared portico. She grasped a large handle at the side of the front door and pulled on it. Somewhere deep inside the house a bell went clang-clang. They could hear Fury barking in the distance, but nothing else happened.

'Are you sure the lady's in?' said Kate, rather hoping that she wasn't.

'Her name's Miss Maine, stupid! She hardly ever goes out. She's half crazy, I think. She doesn't drive any more and her legs are too bad for her to walk far.'

Now the dog's barking sounded closer. Someone must have let him into the house. The front door was a massive affair with lots of small panes of stained glass in it.

The door slowly opened, but only wide enough for someone inside to peek out at them.

'What do you want?' said a quavering voice. 'Go away, or I'll call the police.'

3

'It's only me, Claire,' said Claire, with an I-told-you-so look at Kate. 'I've brought the eggs and a lot of magazines.'

'Who's that with you? I don't know her.'

'It's only my cousin Kate, on a visit.'

There was a fumbling sound and the chain dropped from across the door. A wuffling sound made Kate jump. It was the dog Fury, sniffing at them through the door.

'Come on in, but be quick!' said the voice. The children stepped inside a large, high entrance hall. There was an echoing stone-flagged floor in squares, and a lot of dark pictures on panelled walls. A huge grandfather clock stood silent at the foot of the stairs and the banisters were all twisty with carvings. The place looked as if it could do with a good dusting.

It had a dark, damp feel to it, as if it didn't like fresh air much, and it made Kate feel as if she couldn't breathe properly.

Miss Maine shut the front door and put the chain back on. Kate knew it was rude to stare but she couldn't help it. The old lady looked like a tramp in a stained and faded dress, but her fingers were stiff with rings, set with blue and white sparkling gems. A blazing diamond brooch pinned together the bodice of her dress, where she'd lost some of the buttons.

Her hair was white and she wore what looked like a pink feathered tea cosy on her head. She didn't look any cleaner than her house. She moved with difficulty, walking with the aid of a stick.

Something warm and wet worked its way over Kate's knees, and she squealed.

'It's only Fury,' said Claire. 'You are a scaredy cat, aren't you?'

'Good dog,' said Miss Maine. 'He warned me someone was coming up the hill. I've padlocked the gates because I can't watch them all the time.'

Fury was a large, black Alsatian. Kate supposed he didn't mean any harm and he wasn't actually growling or baring his teeth, but she had the feeling that he might turn nasty at any moment.

Claire said in a sugary voice, 'Kate is very interested in the story about Belle and the ghost. She even dreamed she saw him the other night.'

'When was that?' asked the old lady, in a sharp voice.

'Sunday night,' said Kate. 'But it wasn't a dream.'

'I'll have to report that,' said Miss Maine.

Behind Miss Maine's back, Claire twirled her finger at her temple and pulled a face, meaning she thought the old lady was round the twist.

Miss Maine said, 'Well, little girl, would you like to see my great-grandmother Belle's portrait? Come this way.'

She unlocked a panelled door and ushered the children into a darkened room. Switching on the lights, she pointed to a portrait of a beautiful young girl in a white dress, holding a white rose.

'That was our Beautiful Belle,' said Miss Maine. 'She married a very rich man who took her away to live in a big house in the country. After he died and her elder son got married, she came back here to live with her younger son. That's the portrait of my grandfather, her son, over there.'

She pointed with her stick to a painting of a man with a heavy moustache and a mournful expression. 'He liked to gamble, did my grandfather. You wouldn't think it to look at him, would you? But that's how he spent his time. I can just about remember him. He liked to live in style, but he wasn't much of a businessman, I'm afraid.'

She sighed deeply. 'Over there on the easel is my father.' She pointed to a pastel of a youngish man, also with a moustache, but wearing a soldier's uniform. He had a lot of medals on his chest and looked lively and amused - unlike his father. In a silver frame nearby there was a photograph of the same man looking much older, with a pretty little girl on his knee. Could that possibly have been Miss Maine when she was young? It was hard to believe.

'That was me, with my father. They used to call him the Old Soldier. He was a very brave man.

Grandfather wanted him to marry an heiress to restore the family's fortunes, but when he came back from the war he married a poor schoolteacher instead. They were very happy, but after he died there wasn't much left except this house and some of Belle's pretty things.'

She pointed again with her stick, this time at a large glass dome. 'In there, child, is Belle's bridal headdress. The dome is air-tight, which is why the flowers are so well preserved.'

There was a wisp of white silk veiling in the glass case, and on it rested a circlet of stephanotis and orange blossoms. Kate thought it was weird to keep flowers like that, but was too polite to say so.

This room was airless, too. The shutters were tight over the windows, and heavy curtains had been drawn across them. Everywhere she looked there were flowers, on the carpet, on the curtains, on the tapestry seats of the chairs…but the flowers were all stiff and unnatural. The whole room was unnatural to Kate. You wouldn't ever want to sit on those chairs. Why, you'd slide off, if you tried!

The fireplace was so large and black, it would probably swallow you up, if you got too close.

The house was like a museum.

Miss Maine said, 'This was my great-grandmother's sitting-room. My father liked to keep the old family bits and pieces around him, and so do I. Now that's enough, children. Out you go.'

Miss Maine locked the door of the sitting-room behind her and shuffled off through a door under the stairs. They heard her lock that door behind her, too.

'She's gone to fetch the money for the eggs,' said Claire.

Kate could feel the dog snuffling around her knees again. She wished she'd worn her track suit or her jeans, and not her new pink skirt.

She said, 'Oops, I wish Fury wouldn't do that!'

Claire said, 'You are silly, aren't you?'

Kate said, 'I don't think it's silly to be afraid of large, fierce dogs.'

Claire snatched at Fury's tail. 'I can do anything I like with him. Look!' Fury growled and Claire laughed.

'I don't think he likes that,' said Kate, taking a step back.

Claire did it again. Fury turned on her, the hairs bristling on the back of his neck. Claire recoiled and caught her heel on the bottom step of the staircase. She slipped and fell sideways. At the same time Fury leaped at her, throwing her backwards to the floor. Claire fell awkwardly and then, stupidly, tried to hit the dog out of her way.

Fury planted his paws firmly on Claire's shoulders and began to bark.

Claire screamed.

Kate was paralysed with fear. At any moment she expected Fury to bite great chunks out of Claire. Dogs like that were trained to attack and to bite. Kate had by this time retreated so far that she bumped against the front door.

She could undo the chain and run down the hill and away to safety...or she could stay and help Claire.

No, she couldn't help Claire. Why should she? Claire hated her, and had been horrid to her. Claire had tried to drown her.

Of course, if her daddy had been there, he would have tackled the dog straight away. Her daddy was a hero, but Kate knew that she wasn't any kind of heroine. Then Kate remembered Eloise, saying that she prayed for Claire. She thought of what Eloise had told her about God, and about his son Jesus who liked to listen to us when we asked him for help.

Kate knew she ought to try to help Claire. She also knew she wasn't brave enough, on her own.

'Please, Jesus. Help me!'

Her mind cleared. She still felt afraid, but she could see what she might be able to do to help Claire.

She ran across the hall and seized Fury's collar, pulling with all her strength. 'Bad Fury!' she said. 'Come away!'

Fury was so strong that Kate wasn't sure she could hold him, but at least Claire wasn't being held down on the ground any longer.

Claire wriggled and squirmed out from under Fury, while Kate fought to hold the dog back.

'Down, Fury!' said the old lady, returning with a purse in her hand.

The dog went limp and lay down, panting.

'He attacked me!' cried Claire, almost crying with rage and fear.

'You must have teased him,' said Miss Maine. 'I remember you tried that last week, till I stopped you. You were lucky that your friend kept her head.'

'Look at this!' Claire held out her jacket, which she had caught on a twisty bit of staircase and which had ripped by the armhole. 'You should have stopped him earlier, Kate! You could have done if you had wanted to! Now look what you've done!'

Kate was beyond speech. Reaction made her wobble all over and she leaned against the wall to recover.

'Are you all right, girl?' asked Miss Maine. Kate nodded, and Miss Maine patted her shoulder. 'You're a brave girl. I shall report your behaviour to the proper authorities.'

Kate knew Miss Maine was crazy, but it was nice to be praised for a change. She smiled at the old lady and tried not to mind that an unpleasant smell hung around her.

As luck would have it, Aunty Pat came home for lunch that day, and of course she noticed the tear in Claire's jacket as soon as the girls walked in.

Claire said, 'It was all Kate's fault.'

'Oh dear,' said Aunty Pat, looking distressed. 'Oh, Kate, I wish you'd be more careful. That's a nasty tear and it was a very expensive jacket.'

Kate said, 'It really wasn't my fault, honest!'

'Don't argue with me, Kate,' said Aunty Pat.

'I'll mend it,' said Eloise, pouring oil on troubled waters as usual. 'There is some special stuff, you iron it on to the material, and it shows very little after.'

'Thank you, Eloise,' said Aunty Pat, but she gave Kate a cold look.

Kate was so upset she wanted to burst into tears and stamp out of the room but Eloise caught her eye, and Kate told herself to calm down. It wasn't all the world if people misunderstood her and if Claire wanted to twist everything, then let her! Thank goodness, thought Kate, she only had to put up with Claire for a few days.

Claire's special friend, Tracy, came to play that afternoon. Tracy was taller than Claire and not so pudding-faced, but she looked bored all the time. As soon as she arrived, Claire started to tell Tracy that Kate was a scaredy cat and had got Claire into trouble up at the big house.

Kate clenched her fists and wished she'd never interfered. It would have served Claire right if Fury had savaged her to death. Catch Kate ever helping Claire again!

Tracy offered some gum to Claire but not to Kate. 'Do we have to play with her, then?'

Claire sighed. 'Mum says we've got to. That stupid Eloise has the afternoon off. Mum's going to work in the dining-room and says she wants peace and quiet, so we've all got to go out and play in the garden.'

Aunty Pat's garden was neat and tidy, even in the autumn when there are usually fallen heaps of leaves lying round. You can have a lot of fun jumping and rolling in soft heaps of fallen leaves. Kate always helped her daddy brush them into plastic bags to rot down for compost. Kate's job was to sit on the leaves, to squash them down in the bags. She thought it was odd about leaves; they were ever so light when you picked them up, but when they were squashed down in bags, they soon got too heavy for you to lift.

There were no leaves in this tidy garden. The bushes were all evergreen and the garden was surrounded by an old stone wall. The only trees were the pines that whispered in the wind.

There weren't any good places to play hide and seek in the garden and there was a big bed of heathers in the middle of the lawn which meant you couldn't really play ball games, either.

Kate followed the others as they dawdled along. The garden sloped upwards to the stone wall at the top. Behind a prickly hedge of holly there was the only bit of uncultivated ground, which had once been a vegetable patch. Here there was a sturdy shed, a dump for garden refuse and four more pine trees. When Kate looked back at Aunty Pat's house, she saw she was almost on a level with the roof.

'It's so boring here,' said Tracy, kicking at a stone.

'Could we have a bonfire?' asked Kate, looking hopefully at the rubbish dump. She loved making bonfires, dodging the smoke and prodding pieces of unburned refuse into the heart of the fire.

The other two looked at her as if she were a piece of dirt. Claire said, 'Don't you know anything? Bonfires are bad for the ozone layer. Do you want to bring on global warming?'

Kate was pretty sure that Claire had got this wrong because her daddy had said that it was quite all right to have a bonfire where they lived, though you couldn't in some towns. Her daddy hadn't thought that having a bonfire would bring on global warming and her daddy was always right.

'I suppose,' said Claire, 'we could rig up the badminton net and play with the frisbees.'

'Boring, boring!' chanted Tracy.

Claire brightened up. 'Let's balance a plank across the rubbish dump, run up it and then topple down the other side.'

'Or,' said Tracy, 'we could put the plank up against the wall and drop down into the alley. Then we could go down into the town without your mother knowing anything about it.'

'Yes, let's!' said Claire, jumping up and down.

Kate knew that if she wanted to keep in with these two, she would have to go along with their plan, but she just couldn't do it.

She said, 'No, we mustn't do that.'

'You mean you're afraid.'

'Maybe,' said Kate. But you know we mustn't. Couldn't we have a bonfire? We're allowed to at home.'

'Well, we're not allowed here,' said Claire. To Tracy she added, 'You see what a scaredy cat she is!'

Tracy whispered something in Claire's ear and both girls giggled. They looked at Kate and then looked away. Kate went red. She guessed they were plotting against her.

'I know what we'll do,' said Claire with a grin and a sidelong glance at Tracy. 'We'll climb up onto the wall and pretend we're mountaineers. There's nothing wrong in that, is there?'

Now the wall round the outside of the garden was mostly in good repair, but this one stretch between Aunty Pat's place and the garden of the big house had been neglected. The coping had gone, and several of the big stones had crumbled away to sand.

Claire put a foot here and a foot there, grasped a big stone on the top and hauled herself up. Tracy followed her.

'Come on, Kate,' said Claire. 'There's a marvellous view of the town from up here.'

'It doesn't look very safe,' said Kate.

'It isn't,' said Claire, laughing. 'That's why it's such good fun.'

Kate scrabbled to put her feet in the right places and hauled on the big stone at the top, but slipped and fell back to the ground again. She wasn't any good at this sort of thing. She'd always been afraid of heights and when she looked down between her legs, she could see the ground of Aunty Pat's garden way below her. It sloped away so much that if she fell, she thought she'd roll and roll and maybe hurt herself quite badly.

Suddenly there were screams from above her head. She looked up, but there was no sign of either Claire or Tracy.

Kate panicked. What should she do? Run back to the house for help? The shed and the shrubs hid the house from view.

'Claire! Tracy! Are you hurt? Shall I go for help?'

There was no reply. Kate listened with both ears stretched. If the girls had hurt themselves in their fall, surely they wouldn't both be too badly injured to cry out?

She looked at the wall, towering above her. She could never manage to climb it.

But if the girls were injured, she supposed she must at least try. Kate might not be able to love Claire, but she supposed she could at least see that she didn't die of broken limbs or internal injuries.

Taking a deep breath, she went at the wall again. She grazed her right hand. Tears came to her eyes but she struggled on, trying not to think about the steep drop beneath her.

Finally she pulled herself up to sit on the top and look into the garden of the big house.

Talk about over-grown! It was a forgotten garden, the sort of garden that grew up around the enchanted castle in the story of the Sleeping Beauty. There were huge brambles flying through the air, criss-crossing what had once been paths. There were dark caverns under rhododendron bushes and they grew higher than any bushes she'd ever seen before.

There were more pine trees, and their whispering seemed even louder than before… '…s-stranger beware! S-stranger beware!'

Where were Claire and Tracy? Had the garden swallowed them up? Everything connected with the big house seemed threatening to Kate. She could easily imagine the girls falling into this secret place and lying there dead, with the long grasses covering their bodies for ever and ever. Or perhaps Fury had attacked them and dragged their bodies away.

Was she going to have to jump down, actually to set foot in the garden? She didn't think she dared.

She looked down and right underneath where she sat, she saw that someone had dragged a couple of crates together to form a rough step. It wasn't so far to the ground on this side of the wall. But there was still no sign of the girls. Or of the dog.

Kate dropped down onto the crates and as she straightened up, she caught sight of Tracy's jeans, as her leg slid out of sight beneath a great tangle of bushes. Kate pulled a branch aside and there were Claire and Tracy, killing themselves with laughter.

'Your face!' screamed Tracy.

'I didn't know we were allowed to play here,' said Kate, torn between relief that they were unharmed and anger at the trick they'd played on her. 'What about Fury?'

'He's shut up in the house in the afternoons while Miss Maine has a nap. It's quite all right, so long as you don't go blabbing to Mum about it. She's forbidden us to climb the wall and play here, but that's just being silly. No one ever comes into this part of the garden and we can do what we like here in the afternoons. Come on, let's play hide and seek.'

4

Kate could understand why Aunty Pat had forbidden Claire to climb the wall and play in someone else's garden, but they were there now, and the girls were running away from her, crying to her to count ten and follow them. It was an exciting place to play, a place for real adventure games, for pretending to be explorers in the jungle…

Kate counted ten and ran after the others into a shrubbery which was so dense it shut out the light of the sun. She couldn't see them anywhere at first, and then she heard Tracy giggle, and saw the girls shoot out of the bushes and turn a corner behind an overgrown hedge. Kate followed, and found herself in a neglected kitchen garden, where plants grew taller than herself and seeds showered on her as she brushed through.

The others led her through and out into a wild place and Kate ran after them. They twisted and turned, and so did Kate. At first she quite enjoyed it, but then she got her foot stuck. She'd strayed into a marshy area, and her shoe was firmly embedded in the mud. She could feel the earth sucking at her, trying to pull her into itself. Ugh!

She called out to the girls to wait for her, but of course they didn't. Then it stopped being exciting and became rather frightening.

She got her shoe out and looked round. Suddenly she didn't feel at all safe. It was beginning to get dark. The trees had turned black and were leaning over to look at her again. The bushes seemed to be squatting there, looking at her, waiting for her to fall down and die and be buried for ever.

'Whoo-hooo!'

Was that an owl?

'Eee-eek!'

Was that a bat, squeaking? Kate hated bats. She was always scared that they might tangle with her long hair. She put both her hands over her head to protect herself.

'Whooo-hooo!' There it came again.

Kate swung round, looking up at the trees for the owl. The bat squeaked nearby and she jumped.

All her anxieties rushed back into her mind. Suppose her mummy was worse!

Suppose her daddy had been trying to telephone her, and she hadn't been there! If only she'd stayed in Aunty Pat's garden, where she could have been called to the phone straight away! Here in this terrible place, her daddy could be ringing and ringing, and she'd never know!

'Whooo-heee!' said the owl, but this time Kate didn't jump because that wasn't the way owls hooted. Was that a giggle? The girls must have hidden nearby, and were trying to frighten her again.

One thing was for sure, she had better get back home as quickly as possible. Now she came to look around her, she wasn't entirely sure which way she ought to go. She decided that if she kept going down hill, she must strike the boundary wall at some point. Brambles criss-crossed the paths, and the bushes seemed to have grown even taller and more menacing than she remembered. But she kept on. She slipped on some wet grass, and fell.

She thought the garden was showing that it didn't like her, any more than she liked it. She must get out, quickly. She began to run, and was trapped by a huge bramble, catching hold of her with its thorny fingers.

She freed herself and ran on…and on…and came to some smashed-up greenhouses she'd never seen before. She stopped short and said a little prayer for help. She began to retrace her steps. She could see where she'd beaten down the grass and weeds as she'd raced along. Now and then she came across other tracks in the grass and decided they'd probably been made by Fury. It was a scary thing, being lost in this huge, strange place.

At last she came to the boundary wall and followed it. Sometimes she had to make a detour round shrubs, but she kept on till finally she caught sight of the two crates. She scrambled up onto the top of the wall and looked down into Aunty Pat's garden. There was no sign of the girls, but there was fresh mud on the crates and on the top of the wall, so presumably they'd already gone back home.

It seemed a long way down to the ground. Kate closed her eyes and dropped down, tumbling over at the bottom. She brushed herself down and ran to the house. Sure enough, Claire and Tracy were already there, eating their tea.

'What kept you?' asked Claire.

Kate gave her such a look! But she was too worried about her mummy to argue. She went to her aunt and said, 'Please, have you heard from Daddy? Is Mummy all right? I haven't heard anything for two whole days!'

Aunty Pat said, 'Your father rang. I called and called up the garden, but you didn't come. That was very naughty of you, Kate, wasn't it?'

'Sorry,' said Kate, not knowing how to explain. 'What did he say?'

Aunty Pat took Kate into the dining-room and closed the door. Kate knew then that it was bad news.

'You must be brave,' said Aunty Pat. 'He said your mother was having an operation this afternoon. He said not to tell you unless you asked. He said he'd ring us as soon as he knew she was going to be all right.'

'But suppose…'

'We must hope for the best, that's all. Now run along and have your tea with the others.'

'I don't think I want any tea,' said Kate.

She tore upstairs and fell on her bed. She didn't

want to cry, exactly, but she did want to be alone. She lay there, feeling absolutely dreadful. She wanted to pray, but somehow she didn't seem able to do so.

The door opened and Eloise came in, carrying a plate of biscuits and a mug of milk.

'Oh, Eloise!' Kate found herself crying.

'My poor little one,' said Eloise. She took Kate in her arms and rocked her to and fro. 'We must pray for your mummy, no?'

'I can't. I've tried and I can't. And if Claire says anything, I'll hit her!'

'What has Claire done now?'

'She teased me. She and Tracy. They called me names and tricked me into doing something they knew was wrong and then they tried to scare me and I was frightened and I didn't know what to do. And don't tell me I have to love her, because she's just horrible and I won't, so there!'

'Per'aps that is why you can't pray. Because you 'ave so much hate in you.'

Kate blew her nose and thought about it. It might be true. She did feel hard and nasty inside whenever she thought about Claire and somehow that hard feeling had got all tangled up with the fear she felt about her mummy and the operation.

'You feel bad about your mummy,' said Eloise, 'and that makes it easy for Claire to be a tease. Claire feels bad about her daddy and so she wants to hurt other people, to make them as miserable as she is. Try to understand, yes?'

47

Kate sighed. 'But she is really awful, you don't know how awful.'

'We will pray to Jesus to help us love 'er, and not to hate.'

Kate broke away from Eloise, and stamped her foot. 'I can't! I won't! I want my mummy!'

Eloise knelt down beside Kate, and took her in her arms again.

'I will pray, and you will pray, now. Dear Jesus, you know all the bad thoughts we 'ave, that we hate where we should love. In your love, 'elp us to love and understand, and forgive...as we wish to be forgiven...Kate, say "amen".'

'I suppose so,' muttered Kate.

'Dear Jesus, we also pray for Claire and her mother and her father, in their difficult time. Bring them to love you, too. Kate...'

'All right,' said Kate. 'Amen. I suppose.'

'And dear Jesus, be with Kate's mummy and 'elp the doctors to make 'er well. Comfort and 'elp Kate and 'er father.'

'Amen!' said Kate, really meaning that.

Eloise and Kate sat on the bed while Kate drank her milk and ate the biscuits. They didn't talk. Kate was still anxious about her mummy, but she felt a lot calmer. That must be because of Eloise and her prayers. Perhaps Eloise was right, and Kate had been keeping Jesus away from her while she'd let herself hate Claire. There was a lot to think about.

Eloise asked if Kate would like to go downstairs

and watch the telly, but Kate said she'd like to be quiet and read a book.

It shouldn't have seemed strange, but she was surprised to find that the book she picked up was all about being brave when you were frightened, and how good friends can help you cope.

She tried to go to sleep, but couldn't. Too much had happened that day for her to be easy in her mind.

She heard the phone ring downstairs and knew for absolute certain that it was her daddy. She shot out of the room and hung over the banisters.

Aunty Pat looked up, saw her, and smiled. 'Your mother's going to be just fine.' She held the phone out to Kate.

'Kate, is that you?' said her daddy. 'It's going to be alright. They operated early this afternoon and your mummy's come through it very well. In fact, she's just been sitting up, having a cup of tea and asking how you were. She should he home in a few days. Isn't that good?'

'Oh yes!' said Kate. She wondered why she wanted to cry, when everything was going to be all right.

'I'll be over to see you tomorrow afternoon. We'll go out somewhere, shall we? Claire too, of course.'

'Oh no, Daddy. Please not with Claire. Just the two of us.'

'All right, poppet, whatever you say. Now hand me back to your aunty, will you?'

It was going to be all right! Kate danced all the way back up to her room and knelt down by her bed to thank Jesus. She promised him that she'd really truly try not to hate Claire any more, even if it did seem rather impossible. In fact, Kate thought it would take a miracle.

It was only when she was getting into bed that she remembered Jesus was supposed to be rather good at miracles...which made her laugh for the first time for days.

Kate's daddy arrived promptly on the dot of two and they went off together to a big park on the other side of town, to play on the swings and roundabouts and climbing frames. Kate thought that she was really getting almost too old for such baby playgrounds, but she didn't mention that to her daddy because he was so pleased that he'd found somewhere for her to play. Anyway, the big swings and climbing frames were quite good in their way.

Then they had a really grown-up treat. They went to a big hotel in the High Street and had a special tea for two in the lounge.

There were home-made scones and pats of butter and several kinds of jam, each in its own little pot. There was a big plate of cakes, some with icing on and some with real cream inside. The china had a pretty blue and white pattern on it, and the teapot and hot water jug matched. Kate and her daddy sat at a small table near a beautiful big log fire and it was like being in a marvellous day-dream.

Kate poured out the tea. She wasn't sure about filling up the teapot with hot water straight away or leaving it till later, but her daddy helped her decide.

She had both her scones and one of his. Then she had two cream cakes before she felt full. After that she sat back in her chair and looked about her. The news of her mummy was good and Kate felt marvellous.

'A pity Claire couldn't come,' said Daddy. 'I did hear she'd been going through a difficult patch, missing her father and so on.'

'That's what Eloise says,' said Kate darkly, 'but I don't think that's any excuse. I hate her. I've tried not to, but it doesn't work.'

Her daddy blinked. 'Who's Eloise, and what's Claire been up to?'

'Eloise is Aunty Pat's au pair. She's lovely and she wants me to pray for Claire but I just can't.'

'Tell me about it.'

So Kate told him. She told him about Tomkin and Belle, and Claire saying Kate had imagined the shadow when she hadn't. And about Claire trying to drown her in the baths and not being in the least sorry. And about going up to the big house and meeting the dog, and Claire blaming Kate for the tear in her jacket when it had been all her own fault. And about Tracy and Claire tricking Kate into going over the wall into the garden of the big house when they knew it was forbidden; and how they'd played tricks to scare her and they were just so horrible he couldn't imagine.

51

By this time Kate was nearly crying, she was so sorry for herself.

'Couldn't I come home with you now, Daddy? I'd be ever so good, I promise. Only I don't think I can bear to go back to Aunty Pat's. I'd rather die!'

Kate's daddy stirred his tea and said nothing. Kate blew her nose and settled herself back in her chair. She'd made up her mind and that was that. She was not going back to Aunty Pat's.

Kate's daddy said, 'I wish I could split myself into two. I know you need me, Kate, but at the same time I think I ought to be with your mother at the hospital. And we're so busy at work…there's a meeting I ought to be at, right at this very minute.'

A lump formed in Kate's throat. He meant she was being a nuisance.

'I love you so much, Poppet,' he said, putting his arm around her. 'And I love your mother. And I love my work. You see my problem?'

Kate refused to see it. She knew what she wanted and that was to go home. Anything else was unthinkable.

'Kate, if you were ill and in hospital, your mother and I would let everything else go hang, to be with you. Wouldn't we?'

'Yes,' she said, reluctantly.

'We can't leave you alone in the house all day. I've been in touch with your best friend's Mum and they will be back home on Sunday. They want you to go to stay with them until Mummy comes out of hospital and feels she can cope. I know you're not happy at Aunty Pat's. She told me so on the phone last night and that's why I've come over here this afternoon to be with you, even though I want to be with your mother in hospital at the same time.'

'You can see her this evening,' said Kate.

'Yes. I will. But what am I to tell her, Kate? That you've let a bit of teasing get you down?'

'It's all very well for you,' said Kate, angry to tears. 'You don't know what Claire's like. She's horrid! She enjoys making me cry! If you really loved me, you wouldn't make me go back there.'

'I agree it's not ideal, but you seem to have made friends with Eloise, and she'll look after you.'

'Yes, but there's nothing Claire and I can talk about. She doesn't understand me and she makes fun of me because I get scared of things.'

'There are different sorts of courage, Kate. Some people have very little imagination and until they've experienced fear themselves, they don't understand it in other people. You have lots of imagination and at the moment you are letting your fears get the better of you.'

Kate kicked the leg of the table. 'You don't understand, either.'

'Yes, I do. I've got your sort of imagination, Kate, and I often have to struggle with fear.'

'But you're really brave! You got a medal for it!'

'I'll let you into a secret. When I saw that boy at the window of the burning house, I was so afraid I nearly ran away. Then I thought that if it had been my child, I wouldn't have stood by and watched while he died. So I went in there and got the child out...and as you know, I was hardly burned at all.'

Kate hadn't known grown-ups could be afraid. First Eloise, and now her daddy! This needed thinking about.

She said, 'You mean, I've got to be brave and go back to Aunty Pat's, knowing that Claire will go on being horrible to me? I don't think I can.'

'I'd like you to try again, Poppet, not only because there's nowhere else for you to go, but because you are being given a chance here to prove yourself.'

'Ugh!' said Kate. 'I don't know which is worse, going back to stay with Claire, or diving into a burning house to rescue someone.' She felt a little better now. Even slightly hungry again.

'Go on, have another,' said her daddy, and pushed the plate towards her. Kate took a lovely squishy meringue with real cream in it...yummy, yummy.

She said, 'Could we take back a present for Claire and Aunty Pat?'

'A good idea. A fresh start, right?'

Claire refused to touch the lovely box of fudge there Kate had chosen for her, saying she didn't like that sort of thing at all.

Kate nearly burst with rage. After all her good intentions! It was too much!

Aunty Pat came into the room and said, 'Oh dear, we don't eat sweets in this house, Kate. I ought to have told you.'

Kate thought that Aunty Pat couldn't know about Claire's secret hoard of sweets in the bedroom cupboard.

'By the way, Kate,' said Aunty Pat. 'Claire says that you've been climbing the wall and going into Miss Maine's garden to play. You are never to do that again, understand?'

'Yes,' said Kate, with scarlet cheeks. Claire wasn't playing fair - again.

Eloise came in and exclaimed, 'What lovely sweets! May I 'ave one, Kate? 'ow kind you are!'

Kate threw her arms around Eloise and hugged her, feeling that she was the only person in the house who understood her.

5

Next morning Claire and Kate were sent out into the garden to play again. Aunty Pat had gone off to the office and Eloise was working at her English language homework.

Kate wanted to keep strictly to herself, perhaps watch out for birds. She tried to ignore Claire but Claire didn't intend to be ignored.

Claire pushed Kate, trying to make her fall over.

'Stupid thing!' cried Claire. 'I don't see why I should have to put up with you!'

Kate marched up to the top of the garden to get out of Claire's way. She was beginning to hate Claire again. She knew she shouldn't, but she couldn't help it. Claire ran at Kate again, but this time Kate was ready for her. They pushed and pulled at one another and in the struggle Kate's scarf fell off. Claire swooped on it, bundled it up and threw it over the wall into Miss Maine's garden.

'You rotten thing!' cried Kate. 'Now look what you've done!'

She had a matching red beret, scarf and mittens,

which her mother had given her for her last birthday.

'Go and get it!' cried Claire, laughing fit to burst. 'Go and fetch it, and then I'll tell on you, see if I don't!'

Kate was so mad that she didn't think twice. She scrambled up the wall, holding on here and there, and not even looking down to worry about the drop into the garden below. She got to the top and balanced there, looking for her scarf. It was such a bright red, she couldn't possibly miss it.

Yes, there it was lying on the grass beyond the crates.

But something else was lying on the grass, a little further off.

Kate screamed.

'What is it, stupid?' said Claire. 'Are you so frightened, you can't even jump down to get your scarf?'

'Oh, fetch Eloise, quickly!'

'I'm not going to do that, stupid! She'd tell on us, for sure!'

'It's desperate! Come and see for yourself!'

'What, climb up there? Then you'll push me over, I suppose. I should be so daft!'

'I won't, I promise!'

Claire scrambled up, and saw for herself.

'It's Fury,' said Kate. She was trying to keep calm, but her heart was racing away. 'At least, I think it's him. He's thrashing about and moaning. He must be ill. Quick, fetch Eloise!'

'Don't be silly,' said Claire. 'We can't tell anyone, or they'll know we've been on the wall.' She dropped back into their own garden. 'Someone else will hear him. The old lady will come down the garden and find him. We don't need to bother.'

'There's nobody else's garden overlooks this bit, is there? And you said Miss Maine never comes down into this part of the garden. We have to tell.'

'Don't be daft! You don't know what my mother's like when she's angry. She might stop my pocket money! She'd certainly stop me watching telly tonight and it's Top of the Pops, remember!'

Kate wavered, because she adored Top of the Pops herself. Then she thought about what her mummy and daddy would have done. Her daddy wouldn't have left an animal lying there in pain, just because he might get into trouble for it. Kate remembered how he'd looked after her mummy. Now it was Kate's turn to look after someone else.

Kate said, 'I'll tell, if you like. Then you won't get punished.'

'I shall tell Mummy I wasn't anywhere near. I'll say it was you who threw your own scarf over, to give yourself an excuse to go over the wall.'

'Claire, I think you're the meanest, nastiest girl I've ever met. Tell her what you like. I don't care. I'm going to fetch Eloise.'

Kate jumped down off the wall - and this time it didn't seem impossibly high - and ran down the garden to find Eloise.

'Oh, Kate!' said Eloise, when she had heard the

story, ''ave you been on the wall again? You know it is not safe!'

'Yes, but hurry, please! I'm sure the dog is dreadfully sick.'

Eloise ran up the garden and stood on a wheelbarrow to peer over the wall. Being tall, she didn't need to climb onto the wall itself.

Claire said, grinning, 'I told Kate not to go on the wall. I told her you'd be angry!'

Eloise said, 'The dog is very sick, yes. We must find a vet, quick, quick! But I do not know the name…'

'We could look in the yellow pages of the directory,' said Kate. 'That's what my daddy did when we bought Nibbles and he need injections.'

Eloise took Kate by the hand and together they ran back to the house and found the name of a vet in the directory. They were lucky, because the vet was the same one who looked after Fury, and he knew all about Miss Maine and her odd ways.

He told Eloise to meet him at the front door of the big house. The vet said Miss Maine had got so peculiar lately that she wouldn't let anyone into the house or garden, so Eloise must prepare Miss Maine for the bad news, so that she would know what to expect when the vet arrived.

Kate and Claire raced up the alley with Eloise and knocked on the front door of the big house. They rang the bell too, but nothing happened.

'Perhaps she's died,' said Claire, looking pleased.

At length the door opened a crack. 'Who is it?'

said Miss Maine, in a quavering voice. 'I have a fierce dog here and if you don't go away, I'll turn him loose on you!'

'It's Eloise and Claire,' said Eloise. 'Fury is at the bottom of your garden, and 'e is very, very sick. I have phone the vet, and 'e is coming quick, quick.'

'I don't believe you, girl. Go away. It's all a trick to get me to open the door. Go away, or I'll call the police.'

'Oh, please, Miss Maine!' cried Kate. 'You remember me, don't you? I came the other day with Claire. I saw Fury at the bottom of your garden and he's in a terrible state. Won't you let us in?'

'You are telling lies, bad girl! Fury is right here with me.'

'Then why isn't he barking, as he usually does?'

'Go away, all of you!' cried Miss Maine, and she was just closing the door when a van drew up in the driveway. A big man got out and came to the door.

'Miss Maine, I hear Fury's in trouble. You remember me, don't you? I gave Fury his injections and treated him when he cut his paw.'

He spoke to the old lady through a crack in the door and then straightened up, and turned to the others.

'She doesn't want to let us into the house, but if we go round to the side door that leads onto the terrace, she'll let us into the garden so that we can find Fury.'

He led the way round the side of the house to the first green door, and the others followed. Miss Maine opened the side door just long enough to let them in, and then padlocked it again.

She said, 'I'm not leaving the house. I'm being spied on, you know.'

Claire giggled and made a screwing motion with her forefinger at her temple but the vet knew how to treat Miss Maine and merely nodded.

'Don't worry, Miss Maine. The children will show me the way.'

'I don't know where Fury is,' said Claire, with her chin in the air.

Eloise said, 'Kate, can you show us the way?'

Kate looked around her but couldn't recognise anything. They were standing on what had once been a stone-paved terrace with a fountain in the middle of it, but it was so overgrown you could hardly see the stones for weeds. Below lay what once had been a rose garden, with the odd bloom poking up. A bank of shrubs lay beyond that.

'I don't know where it is,' said Kate miserably. 'I've only been over the wall once and I got lost then. All I know is, I could see the dog lying in the long grass near the wall at the top of our garden.'

'And you live…where?' said the vet.

'In Pine Tree Close,' said Eloise.

'Right,' said the vet. 'Well, if we go down the garden keeping the boundary wall on our right, we should strike the place.' He led the way down an overgrown path and through a dense shrubbery. The wind was rising and the pine trees were beginning to rustle and whisper to themselves. Rain spat into Kate's face, and she shivered. She missed her nice warm scarf.

They came to the marshy place, stumbled past the smashed-up greenhouses, trailed through the forlorn vegetable garden and then went around a bramble patch to the wall. They found the crates and Kate's scarf, but no dog.

'You see,' said Claire. 'Kate made it all up. She is such a liar.'

'But I saw the dog also,' said Eloise 'It was here, I promise you.'

Kate picked up her scarf and tied it securely around her neck. Only then did she see something on the ground under a bush, and pointed.

'I think he's in there.'

The vet pushed aside the bushes and there was Fury, shivering, and trying to burrow away from the light.'

'He's been sick,' said the vet, 'and he is certainly not well. Ahha…' He took some special gloves out of his bag and, picking something up out of the grasses, placed it carefully in a plastic envelope. It looked like a piece of raw meat to Kate.

The vet straightened up and said to Eloise, 'Will you take the children back up to the house and ask Miss Maine to open the side door again so that I can carry the dog up and put him straight in my van?'

Claire wanted to stay and watch but Kate couldn't bear the sight of the poor dog's suffering, and was glad to get away. They found Miss Maine on the terrace. She was talking to herself at a great rate, and they could hardly make her listen.

'Dirty spies, spying on me, all the time,' she was saying. 'I've told them over and over, but they don't believe me...no one ever believes me...'

The vet carried Fury up the garden in his arms, waited for Miss Maine to unlock the terrace door, and put him in the van while Miss Maine turned the key in the padlock behind them.

As the van drove away down the hill Eloise said, 'Well, that is over. Now we must think what nice thing to do with our day. 'ow about going to the cinema this afternoon, yes?'

They went to see a Disney film. They had all seen it before, but they enjoyed seeing it again. Now and again Kate thought about poor Fury, and wondered if he were all right. She also worried about what Aunty Pat would say when she heard that Kate had been climbing the wall again. She didn't think Claire would take her share of the blame.

Claire didn't.

Aunty Pat was putting her car away in the garage as they got back from the cinema. It was getting dark and still drizzling.

'There's a funny thing,' said Aunty Pat. 'Two policemen have just been down the alley with torches. They were poking around the hedge and all along the wall, checking to see if someone had left any raw pieces of meat out for neighbourhood cats and dogs. They said Miss Maine's dog has been poisoned. I told them she's half crazy and probably gave the dog some contaminated meat herself, without realising what she was doing.'

'Ah, of course,' said Eloise, looking relieved. 'That would be the explanation. These old ladies, they get careless when they cook.'

'Oh!' said Kate. 'You mean that she might have thrown some bad meat over our wall? Why, Nibbles might have found some and eaten it! Is he all right?'

They had to lock Nibbles into the house very firmly every time they went out, or he dashed out to play in the road. Kate rushed into the house to look for him but Nibbles was perfectly all right, asleep on one of Aunty Pat's jumpers in the sitting-room. Aunty Pat wasn't best pleased to find Nibbles on her jumper because of the hairs, and she was even more annoyed when Claire said Kate had been climbing the wall again.

Eloise tried to make excuses for Kate. 'She 'ad to 'elp the dog...'

Claire said triumphantly, 'I told her you'd be angry.'

'I am angry,' said Aunty Pat and took Kate into the other room for a telling-off. 'Now Kate, did you really climb that wall again? After I told you most specially not to do so?'

'My scarf got thrown over and I climbed up to get it. That's when I saw Fury. I knew you'd be cross, but I couldn't not tell, could I? I mean, poor Fury might have died if I hadn't fetched Eloise and she hadn't got the vet.'

'Do you think that makes it any better?'

'N-no, but...do you think we could ring the vet and find out how Fury is getting on?'

Aunty Pat found the number in the directory and talked to the vet's assistant, who said that Fury was still very weak, but they thought he'd live.

'Oh, good,' said Kate.

'That's all very well, but I really can't overlook your behaviour. You are proving a most troublesome guest, Kate. If your mother were not in hospital, I'd ask my brother to take you home again. As it is, I really don't know what to do with you. I have to go out to work every day, so I can't keep an eye on you all the time. And every time my back is turned, you get up to some mischief or other.'

'I am trying to be good,' said Kate, thinking that she'd like to do something terrible to Claire.

'I daresay. Well, you can go up to your room straight away, now. Eloise may bring you up some tea, but you stay there for the rest of the evening. Naturally there will be no television, nor a story tonight. Understood?'

It made Kate feel dreadful to be scolded, especially when it was mostly Claire's fault that she was in trouble. She hated to miss one of her favourite programmes, too. It was going to be so dull in her bedroom! She stamped up the stairs and slammed the bedroom door behind her. She hated everything!

An hour later there was a bang on the door and Claire walked in with a plate of fish fingers and baked beans, and a mug of orange.

Claire said, 'I didn't want to bring up your supper, but Eloise said I must. Mummy's gone out again but you're not to come down and you're not watching telly, so there.'

'Thank you,' said Kate, taking the plate and mug off Claire. She expected Claire to go away again, but Claire didn't.

'The programme was brill,' said Claire. 'You missed a treat, but that serves you right, doesn't it? For not taking me out with your father.'

Kate choked on a piece of fish finger.

'You've gone all red,' said Claire. 'You do look silly!'

Kate told hold of her plate with both hands and thought about smashing it into Claire's face. How satisfying it would be to spread baked beans all over that silly grin of hers, and get tomato sauce into her hair and down that grown-up glittery sweater she was wearing! How Claire would screech! She would howl and run for her mother and perhaps would even cry! And wouldn't that be cool!

But Kate held back. As clearly as if someone had spoken the word in the room, she heard Eloise say, 'You must try to love Claire…'

Kate weighed the plate in her hand, and argued with herself. Claire didn't deserve to be loved, she was so horrible she needed to be taught a lesson.

'…and are you so good yourself…?'

With an effort Kate turned away, plonked the plate down on her bedside table, and started eating.

Claire laughed, but it wasn't her usual loud laugh. It was a breathless sort of laugh. 'Hey, I thought you were going to throw that plate at me for a minute.'

'Serve you right if I had,' said Kate around a mouthful of baked beans. 'You aren't worth it, though. And I'm hungry.'

Claire went red and pushed her hands into her pockets. 'It's you who aren't worth it! Stupid! Scaredy Cat! Yah!'

Kate hated it when people shouted at her. She began to tremble but she tried to keep her voice steady. 'I have to stay till the end of the week, whether you like it or not...'

'I don't!'

'Well, neither do I like it, but there's nothing we can do about it and I don't see why you should have to make me so unhappy, I really don't!'

'Don't you, then!' said Claire, pushing out her chin at Kate. 'Oh yah, little miss milk-and-water! Is she going to cry, then? Go on! Cry! Why shouldn't you be unhappy, like the rest of us!'

'But you've got your mother...'

'She's never here,' snapped Claire. 'Even when she is, she's thinking about work, or going out to parties. You've seen what she's like.'

'I heard your father had gone away. I'm sorry.'

Claire threw herself headlong on the bed and looked up at the ceiling. She didn't speak and neither did Kate, for a long time.

Kate said at last, 'You have Eloise.'

Claire shrugged. 'She's stupid. She can't even speak English properly.'

'She loves you.'

'Don't be silly. Au pairs don't love people. They work for them. They get paid for it.'

'She said she loved you and prayed for you all the time. She wanted me to pray for you, and to love you, too. But I couldn't, though I did try at first. I can't love you. Not to be honest and true.'

Claire sat up, her face red. 'I don't want you to pray for me or to love me. I hate you!' She rushed out of the room and slammed the door behind her.

6

Kate finished off her supper and had a bath. The house seemed very quiet tonight. Even the telly was off, but from the top floor came the 'ping' and jingle of someone playing a game on a computer. At least Claire was enjoying herself.

It really was very quiet. Too quiet. Perhaps Eloise had gone out, as well as Aunty Pat. That was a scary thought.

There was only one thing for it; she must try to pray. Kate knelt down and said, 'Please Jesus, will you look after Daddy and help Mummy get well quickly. It's pretty awful here, except for Eloise, who is lovely and I'd like her to come to stay and have a good holiday in our house when Mummy gets better. Thank you for making Eloise so nice and thank you for Nibbles. Amen.'

She had a fight with herself. She really didn't want to pray for Claire, not one bit, but she was beginning to realise that Claire needed a lot of help and a lot of loving.

'Well,' said Kate, 'If you're not too busy, Jesus, you know how awful Claire is, and could you do something about it? I'm trying not to hate her, but it's hard work and I could do with some help. Please. Amen.'

Then she got into bed and read some more of her book. The boy in the book was having to cope with all sorts of nasty, spooky things. There were lots of bad people around, and dark corners to be faced, but he was going to come out on top, and the evil would vanish. It gave Kate a nice warm feeling. She wished she were as brave as the boy in the book. Or her father.

She sighed a bit, thinking about how impossible it was to feel brave when there were spooky things about in real life. She supposed she ought to pray about that, too. So she did. And though she didn't much want to, she tried to pray for Claire all over again. This time it came out almost as if she meant it.

Eloise came into the room, smiling. 'Time for turning out the lights? 'Ave you said your prayers?'

'Yes, and for Claire, too.'

Eloise leaned across Kate to draw the curtains more closely across the window and Kate said, 'Do you think I ought to pray about the shadow, too?'

'What is the shadow?'

'I saw something on the path outside and it frightened me. Claire laughed at me and said I'd made it up. That's when she decided I was a coward but I really had seen something, you know. I wasn't asleep, and I hadn't imagined it.'

Eloise looked as if she didn't know what to

think. Kate lifted up a corner of the curtain and looked out, point up the path.

'I saw it…there…oh!'

She screamed and dropped the curtain. 'It's there again…oh!'

Eloise took Kate in her arms. 'There, now. You're trembling!'

'It hasn't got any face, Eloise!'

Eloise pulled back the curtain and looked out. 'There is nothing there, my Kate. Look for yourself.'

Kate took courage and looked out, too. The alley was empty. She was still shivering, so Eloise pulled the curtains close to and gave Kate a cuddle. 'Now, Kate, you will tell me everything.'

'You won't laugh? You will believe me?'

'You are a girl who speaks true, no? I will believe, but you will be careful to say only true, yes?'

'Yes,' said Kate. 'It was the first night I came. It was all dark outside, but the moon was shining and there was that lamp on the corner, going up the path. I was looking at the darkness under the hedge opposite, and part of it broke away and went up the hill. It was like part of the shadow, only it was like a spider, too. A gi-normous spider. It frightened me.'

'You saw a man walk up the 'ill. That path is not much used at night, but sometimes it is a short way for people who live over the 'ill.'

'If it was a man, then it wasn't an ordinary man. He didn't walk straight up the middle of the path as people usually do. He didn't walk upright, either.

He was bending low, so close to the hedge that I thought at first he was a part of it.'

Eloise laughed. 'You thought it was the ghost!'

Kate coloured up. 'Yes, I did, a bit. Aunty Pat had just told us about Tomkin and Belle and I did think at first that it might be the ghost but…it isn't midnight yet. Don't ghosts have to wait till midnight?'

'There are no ghosts, my Kate. That is true, believe me.'

Kate only half believed her. 'But if it wasn't a ghost, what was it and why did it act so strangely?'

'Per'aps it was Miss Maine, bent over on 'er stick.'

'N-no,' said Kate, thinking about it. 'Miss Maine isn't very tall, not as tall as you, but she walks slowly as if her feet hurt and she wears special heavy shoes. She walks plonk, plonk. The shadow walks quick quick like you, but not like you. And his arms swing forward as he walks.'

'You saw a man in black clothes, out for a walk, that's all.'

'Y-yes,' said Kate. 'But then why did he bend so low as he walked, and why did he go so close to the hedge and why…' She stopped and swallowed. '…when I saw him just now, he was coming down the hill, and as I picked up the curtain he lifted his head and looked up at me…only he hadn't got any face!'

Kate burst into tears and buried her head against Eloise, who held her close.

Eloise said, 'I think you 'ave seen a man going

for the jogging, that is all. He would wear a skiing hat, per'aps, with just 'oles for the eyes and the mouth.'

'No holes,' said Kate. 'He hadn't any face at all. It was all white and blurry when he looked up. Eloise, I know I'm a coward, but I am frightened.'

'Always we are frightened of things we do not understand. This will 'ave some reason and we will find it together, no?'

'But how?'

Eloise smiled, meaning that Kate ought to know how.

'We tell Jesus about it,' said Kate, understanding what Eloise meant. 'And we ask him to help us. Right?'

'Very right,' said Eloise.

In the morning something awful happened. Aunty Pat told Eloise to take Claire and Kate swimming again!

Claire was quite happy about this, especially since she immediately sent Tracy a text message to meet her at the baths and Tracy texted back that she would. But poor Kate! Even the thought of going into the water with Claire made her feel ill.

She thought of saying that she felt sick and asking if she could stay at home and play with Nibbles. But Eloise would be taking Claire and Kate knew that Aunty Pat wouldn't let her stay in the house alone.

Kate thought about begging Eloise not to take

them. Perhaps there would be a thunderstorm and they needn't go out. Perhaps ten o'clock need never come.

Then she saw Eloise smiling at her. Eloise knew all about Kate's fear and was telling her what to do about it. So Kate went and gave Nibbles a cuddle and told Jesus all about it, quietly, after breakfast. When Nibbles was tired of playing, Kate helped Eloise stack the dishwasher. Then she tidied her bedroom. She felt she could face whatever happened. Well, almost.

Claire met Tracy outside the baths and they went off together. Eloise jumped down into the water and held out her arms for Kate. Kate hesitated, all her fears returning.

'Shall I get some armbands, Kate?' asked Eloise.

Kate straightened up. Armbands were for babies. She'd been able to do a breaststroke without armbands for a whole term. Eloise must think she was a real baby, and perhaps she was, being so afraid all the time.

She jumped down into the water and splashed across the pool with Eloise at her side. Eloise suggested they had a contest to see who could stay under water the longest. Eloise won, but Kate got so good at it that she forgot about being afraid. Eloise showed Kate how to push herself off the side and float away on her back. Kate liked that, because it meant she could see where she was going so that no one could bump into her unawares.

Tracy and Claire were playing water polo at the

other end of the baths with some of their schoolfriends. It was easy for Eloise to keep an eye on them while helping Kate.

'Time to go 'ome!' cried Eloise.

'Oh, must we?' said Kate. 'I was just getting the hang of it.'

Eloise laughed. 'Per'aps we can come again another day.'

Kate laughed, too. Eloise was teaching her more than how to improve her swimming and Kate knew it.

Claire went to play with Tracy that afternoon, so Kate helped Eloise with the housework. Kate didn't usually help with the housework at home, but Eloise explained to her that when her mummy came out of the hospital, she would be feeling very weak. Eloise said it would help Kate's mummy get well quickly, if Kate were to do some of the jobs around the house. Kate saw the point of that, and learned how to change the duvet covers and undersheets on Aunty Pat's and Claire's beds.

They talked about the shadow again. Eloise said she thought it must be some naughty boy, trying to give everyone a fright. That made Kate feel better, too.

Kate's daddy rang, and asked how she was getting on.

'Better,' said Kate with a sigh. 'But really, Claire is very trying.'

'But you are coping better?'

'A bit. How is Mummy?'

'Getting stronger every day. She was able to walk a few steps today. She worries about you a lot, I'm afraid.'

'Tell her I'm all right,' said Kate, feeling very grown-up for a change. 'Tell her I'm learning a lot of new things, even how to help her with the housework when she gets home.'

'Really, Poppet? Well, that's a turn up for the books.'

Kate giggled, because she could tell how pleased he was with her. She said, 'I wanted to throw my baked beans all over Claire, but I didn't. I've learned how to swim on my back and when I get home I'm going to be able to help Mummy change the sheets and the duvet covers on our beds!'

'That's marvellous, Poppet.' His voice went all deep and she sighed again but this time with pleasure. It was lovely when she got things right.

He said, 'Well, I'll be over to collect you at the weekend. You're to stay with your best friend down the road till Mummy comes out of hospital and probably have your evening meal there as well for a time. You won't mind that, will you?'

'No, that'll be lovely. But you will let me help to look after Mummy a bit, won't you?'

'Darling, that'll be just...' He coughed a bit. Perhaps he was getting a cold. He said, 'Well, you think you can last out, then?'

'Sure,' said Kate. 'With a bit of help from Eloise, you know.'

Kate was helping Eloise get the supper when

Claire came home. Claire had quarrelled with Tracy and was in a very bad mood. She snapped at Kate and even lashed out at Nibbles when he ran up to her, wanting to play.

Kate had been thinking nice thoughts about Claire, but now she went back to hating her. Claire really was the end! Fancy trying to kick Nibbles!

Aunty Pat rang up to say that she wouldn't be back for supper, but was going on to a party somewhere, so Eloise said they should have a special meal all to themselves. Claire said she was going to eat in front of the telly and they could do what they liked, which spoiled things somewhat.

Half way through the evening, Kate began to worry about the shadow. Suppose he came back that night? Suppose he wasn't really a boy playing tricks, but a really truly ghost?

Kate shivered. She gave Nibbles a cuddle, trying to comfort herself as he purred against her. It was all very well saying there was no such thing as a ghost, but if there wasn't, then why did the shadow have no proper face?

She didn't really want to go upstairs when the time came to go to bed. Eloise was gentle but firm. Kate and Claire must go to bed at the usual time, or else! Why, what would happen if Aunty Pat were to come home and find them still watching the telly?

Claire stumped up to her own room and slammed the door. Kate left hers open. She got undressed, washed and climbed into her Snoopy nightshirt. She thought she might as well try to pray, to see if it would help. She knelt down but somehow her heart was beating so hard that she couldn't breathe properly, and she couldn't get her thoughts clear. She knew she ought to be praying for Claire and for her mummy and daddy, but all she could think of was 'Help!'

'What are you doing?' Claire had come into the room behind Kate, and was looking at her as if she were an idiot.

'Praying,' said Kate. She got into bed, feeling silly. Then she told herself not to feel silly, just because of Claire.

'For me, I suppose?' said Claire in a sneering way.

'Trying to,' said Kate. 'Also about the shadow. He really frightens me.'

'Oh, you're frightened of anything. Fancy being scared of a shadow!' Claire leaped onto the bed and parted the curtains to look out. Then she let out a shriek and collapsed. 'Oh, oh! What is it? Oh, I shall die of fright!'

Kate peeped out, holding her breath. There wasn't anybody there.

Claire rolled about, screeching with laughter. 'Oh, your face! You thought I'd seen a ghost but I was having you on! Oh, I shall die laughing!'

'You idiot!' said Kate, angrily. 'You really did frighten me. If you'd seen what I saw...'

'Oh, come off it, scaredy cat!' Claire twitched the curtains apart. 'There's nothing there, and there never was anything there. You are a stupid girl!'

Kate looked and felt something cold crawl down her back. There was something there now. Something, someone...a spidery figure, in the shadows, creeping up the hill...just as he had done before.

'What's that, then?' asked Kate, in a faint voice.

'What?' said Claire. 'Seeing ghosts again, are we?'

'No,' said Kate, still in that strange voice. 'I don't think it's a ghost. I'm going to fetch Eloise.'

She ran out onto the landing and called to Eloise. Eloise had been watching the telly and it was some moments before she heard Kate and came to see what had happened.

Claire was leaning against the window looking out. She said. 'I didn't see anything. It's that stupid girl, making things up again. She screamed for you, Eloise, just to get you away from the telly. Just because she wasn't allowed to watch late tonight.'

'No,' said Kate, her heart beating so hard she could hear it in her ears. 'Eloise, that thing - whatever it is - it went up the path again, just a few minutes ago.'

Eloise struck her hands together. 'I will have words with this stupid boy, frightening you children.'

'He's gone now,' said Kate, peeping out.

'He was never there,' said Claire. 'She imagined it.'

'I do not think that,' said Eloise. 'I think your cousin is speaking true, and she says so much of detail, she could not make it up. We will wait for this silly boy who plays tricks, and I will speak to him very firm when 'e comes back.'

'Now you're both being stupid,' said Claire. 'If there is someone, then it's just some man taking his dog for a walk. Why make such a fuss?'

'Because,' said Eloise patiently, 'the man 'as no face.'

Claire said, 'What do you mean, "no face"?'

'You will see,' promised Eloise. She pulled the curtains right back. She said, 'We cannot see 'im from the downstairs, because there is no other window this side of the 'ouse. We will wait 'ere for 'im.'

'"No face"?' said Claire. 'How can a man have "no face"?'

'I think 'e 'as covered it with something,' said Eloise. 'Per'aps a mask, or a balaclava helmet. That's why I think 'e's up to no good.'

Claire put herself into the corner furthest away from the window. 'Well, of course I don't believe in ghosts, but if he has no face...' She seemed uneasy for the first time, then she took a flying leap onto the bed and peered out. 'Oh, you're both being so stupid. Won't Mummy laugh when I tell her how stupid you've been!'

Kate was surprised at how little frightened she was, now. Of course it did help that Eloise and Claire were in the room with her, but it wasn't just that. She was beginning to trust in this Jesus her father had been talking about, and that made all the difference.

They waited. Claire fidgeted. She said she ought to be in bed, but she didn't go.

Kate and Eloise saw the shadowy figure at the same moment. Kate reached out and gripped Eloise's hand.

The light from their window was streaming out over the alley because the curtains had been drawn back. The figure hesitated at the edge of the lighted area and looked up at their window.

Where his face should have been, there was a pale blank space.

Claire, who had been playing with Kate's pillow, took one look and with a gasp, keeled over and fell to the floor.

Eloise cried out, 'Claire!' and stooped to lift the child back onto the bed. She said to Kate, 'Quick, run and fetch 'elp...knock on the door of one of the other 'ouses!'

Kate couldn't move. If she ran out of the house, the shadow would get her, with its No Face and its spidery arms!

'Run!' cried Eloise. 'Be quick, my Kate...'

'I-I can't!'

'You can, for me, and for Claire!'

For her horrible cousin? Not likely!

Then Kate remembered her father telling her how afraid he'd been at the burning house, and she knew she had to try. She ran out onto the landing and pounded down the stairs. Nibbles appeared from nowhere, wanting to play. Kate tugged at the latch on the front door and got it open. There were cold fingers playing up and down her spine and she didn't feel she could look towards the alley, or the creature would spring out and fasten itself upon her.

She hesitated. She couldn't do it. Eloise had said that we must love one another. Love even Claire.

It wasn't possible to love Claire as she loved her daddy and her mummy and her special friends and Eloise...but she could feel sorry for Claire and want to help her, and perhaps that might do.

She ran out into Pine Tree Close and turned left away from the alley. There were no lights on in the house next to theirs. The people who lived there must be out or away. The next house along had a light in the front room, and Kate ran across to it, fearing at any minute that the spidery creature would leap onto her back...

She was almost at the front door when she heard someone swearing and then came the sound of a fall. With her finger on the doorbell, she looked over her shoulder. She saw that Nibbles had followed her outside and was dancing around the spidery creature, trying to get him to play.

The man - and it was a man, and not a giant spider - was trying to swerve around the kitten, but had dropped something he'd been carrying...and it was rolling away across the Close. It winked and shone as it rolled It was some kind of silver dish.

The spidery man ran after it and as he did so, Nibbles got in his way again. The man aimed a blow at the kitten and as he did so, Kate saw that he was all hunched over with bumpy black plastic sacks…the mouth of one of the sacks had fallen open, and it was from this bundle that the silver dish had fallen…and Kate could see more silver inside.

A big fat man came to the door of the neighbour's house and said 'Yes?' in a cross voice.

Kate pointed to the spidery creature. The man stopped looking annoyed at being interrupted in watching the telly, and shot into action.

He yelled back into the house, 'Milly, dial 999!' And then he went for the spidery creature, who stopped trying to recover the silver dish and turned to run back down the hill.

He was quick and light but Nibbles was quicker and lighter. With one of his fast, darting runs, he got in front of the strange creature and tripped him up.

Splat! Crash! The creature fell headlong into the road and his bundles went every which way. As they fell, so other silver objects trickled out and lay in the light of the street-lamps.

'Gotyer!' said the big man. He sat on the spidery creature, who said 'Ooof!'

That was all he could say, because the breath had all been knocked out of him.

Kate ran to Nibbles, picked him up and cuddled him tightly.

The big man said, 'Let's be having a look at yer, then.' He pulled something up and off the spidery creature's head. The spidery creature had a perfectly ordinary face, now they could see it.

83

'Nylon stocking over the 'ead,' said the big man. 'I thought so. Been doing a spot of burgling, 'ave we? That's a nice bit of silver you've collected. Been up at the big 'ouse? Bothering Miss Maine, I shouldn't wonder.'

7

Two cars shot into Pine Tree Close and parked. The first car was marked 'Police'. Two large men got out and said, 'Well, if it isn't our old friend the Spider!'

They looked really pleased as they took charge of the burglar.

The other car was Aunty Pat's and she didn't look at all pleased.

'What's going on?' she said, in her sharpest voice. When she saw Kate, she got really angry. 'What are you doing out here at this time of night in your nightshirt? You naughty girl! Go back indoors at once!'

'Steady on,' said the big man. 'If it 'adn't been for this little girl and 'er cat, I reckon me laddo 'ere would 'ave got clean away with the stuff. She's a right little 'eroine, she is!'

One of the policemen was picking up the fallen silver dish. 'This yours, missus?' he asked Aunty Pat.

'No, of course not,' said Aunty Pat. 'I think - I'm not sure - but isn't that from Miss Maine's house? Is this man a burglar?'

There was a flurry of explanations, during which Kate remembered that she'd originally been sent out to fetch help for Claire. She tugged at Aunty Pat's sleeve, and was told to be quiet.

'But Aunty Pat, Claire's really upset...'

'I told you to be quiet!' said Aunty Pat. 'How many more times...'

They were interrupted by a shriek from the door. Eloise had brought Claire downstairs, almost carrying her, because Claire was crying so hard she couldn't walk straight.

'Mummy, Mummy, I heard your car!' Claire leaped straight from Eloise into her mother's arms. 'Make the horrid man go away! Mummy, I'm frightened!'

'Don't be silly, Claire,' said Aunty Pat. 'There's nothing to be frightened of.' But all the same Aunty Pat dropped her coat and bag on the ground and knelt down to cuddle her daughter.

One of the policemen said, 'Well, missus, it's no wonder your daughter was frightened. Old Spider Legs here makes a habit of terrifying people, going round with a mask over his face. We reckon he's been responsible for two or three burglaries around and about...but now we've got him cold, and he'll be sent away for a long time - thanks to your other daughter.'

Eloise put her arm around Kate and held her tight. Kate leaned against Eloise, grateful for her understanding. Now the danger was past, Kate was feeling weak and shivery. It was nice to be praised, but it would be even nicer to be tucked up in her own bed at home with Nibbles.

'What's been going on?' asked Aunty Pat, who was still holding Claire. Claire was sobbing so hard she shook in her mother's arms. Aunty Pat looked at Kate and said, 'Have you been upsetting Claire again?'

Eloise said, 'No, Kate 'as been very brave girl. She saw that bad man and she told me. We watched and waited, all three of us. I knew 'e must be bad man, because of the mask 'e was wearing. But when 'e came, Claire was so fright, she went boom! Flat on the floor. So I sent Kate down for 'elp. She was very very fright, but she came down to 'elp Claire...'

'I see,' said Aunty Pat, looking as if she didn't like it much.

'Now,' said Eloise firmly, 'I take Kate up to 'er bed with 'er cat. I give 'er nice hot drink and she goes to sleep. She is very tired and any questions, they will be for the morning, no?'

'Agreed,' said the policeman, smiling. 'We can get a statement from your neighbour here...' he meant the fat man, 'and in the morning maybe we'll have a chat with this brave little girl, too.'

Aunty Pat was so surprised by what had happened that she didn't even object when Eloise and Kate took Nibbles upstairs with them. Kate was so tired she leaned on Eloise all the way up.

Claire had stopped crying by this time and got the hiccups instead. But Aunty Pat looked after Claire and made a fuss of her, so that was all right.

Kate got into bed and Nibbles curled up beside her, just as he did at home. Eloise sat on the bed and said, 'Now we will 'ave a quiet talk with Jesus, no?'

Eloise didn't have to tell Kate what to say this time. They didn't pray aloud, but each of them quietly thanked Jesus for looking after them, thanked him for Nibbles' help, and asked him to be with Claire and her mummy.

Nibbles was purring like a steam engine in Kate's ear. Kate turned herself towards him and fell asleep.

The next day everyone except Nibbles felt rather tired. Aunty Pat even rang up her office and told them she wouldn't be in to work that day, as she was needed at home.

Claire was still inclined to be tearful. She didn't want to talk to Kate or Eloise, or even phone Tracy, but followed her mummy around all the time. Kate thought Aunty Pat would tell Claire to go away and play as she usually did, but Aunty Pat didn't. Instead she took Claire away into the front room and they had a long chat together.

Once Kate and Eloise heard the sound of the telephone bell, and later on Aunty Pat said they'd rung Claire's daddy and he was going to come back on a visit to them soon. So that was good.

The police arrived and took a statement from Eloise and from Kate.

Aunty Pat and Claire joined them in the kitchen to hear the details.

The police said that poor Miss Maine had been aware that someone was watching her house for some time. Living all alone with only the dog for company, she'd been very scared and had been afraid to let anyone into the house - even the girls when they called with the eggs and the magazines.

When Miss Maine heard that Kate had seen a dark figure creeping up the alley, she had reported it to the police. But the police had been so busy with other crimes that they hadn't taken much notice until Fury ate the poisoned meat.

Aunty Pat had been quite wrong to think that Miss Maine might have given Fury bad meat. It had been the burglar, who had wanted to get the dog out of the way before he attempted to break into the house.

With Fury out of the way, the burglar finally managed to break in. Although Miss Maine had locked and padlocked every door and secured every window, the burglar had climbed up a drainpipe at the back of the house and prised open the window of an unused bedroom.

He had been after Miss Maine's beautiful jewellery as well as the silver, but Miss Maine had recently taken to sleeping in a downstairs room, because she had so much difficulty climbing the stairs. She had her jewellery in the downstairs rooms with her, so the burglar had ransacked the bedrooms in vain.

Miss Maine slept very lightly as most old people do. When she heard the burglar moving around above her, she was very frightened, but kept her head. She had been sleeping in a small room near the kitchen quarters, where there was a phone. She wedged a chair under the doorknob so that the burglar couldn't get in, and rang the police.

By this time the burglar had found his way to the dining-room and put all the family silver into his bags. Perhaps he would have gone on to attempt the door of the room in which Miss Maine was, but then he heard the police car arrive. He fled out of a side window down the alley, only to be tripped up by Nibbles in Pine Tree Close.

The police said that if Kate had not been so brave, Fury would probably have died at the bottom of the garden and the burglar might never have been caught. They said that they hoped Kate would be given a reward for it, which made Claire look cross all over again.

'Oh, that poor Miss Maine,' said Eloise. ''ow she must have felt, all alone. Is she all right?'

'Very shaken,' said the policeman. 'She refused to stay in the house all by herself, but made arrangements to go to stay with an old friend. We've seen her again this morning, and she's talking of staying on with her friend permanently, or of moving into a ground floor flat somewhere. I know the council have been wanting to buy her house and grounds for years, so perhaps she'll sell it to them, now.'

'Oh, dear,' said Aunty Pat. 'Does that mean rows of cheap houses and flats next door?'

'No,' said the policeman. 'The council want the house for a museum and community centre, and the garden would be tidied up and become a public park. There isn't one on his side of town, and I think it would be much appreciated. But that's all in the future.'

'Where is Miss Maine staying?' asked Eloise. 'I'd like to visit 'er, to see if she is all right.'

'And me,' said Kate.

Claire sniffed. 'I suppose I ought to go, too.'

'We'll all go,' said Aunty Pat, which surprised everybody. 'We'll take her some flowers this very afternoon.' She gave Kate a really nice smile, too. 'I expect Miss Maine will wish to thank you, Kate. As I do. We didn't quite understand one another at first, did we? But now I've heard the truth about one or two little incidents...' and here she put her arm around Claire and hugged her, '...why, we can forgive and forget, can't we?'

'Of course,' said Kate. It would be hard, but she'd try.

Miss Maine was staying in a house which was almost as grand as her own, but on the other side of town. Her friend was much younger, though, and the house was clean and sweet-smelling.

There was a nice bright gas log fire in the grate, and all the chairs were comfortable. Miss Maine had spent the morning resting and had borrowed some clean clothes from her friend, so she looked like an ordinary person instead of a tramp, for once. Her jewellery sparkled as much as ever, but she was still shaky after her adventure.

She repeated what the policemen had said. She had decided never to go back to her old home. She was too old now to live alone. Her friend would like to have her to stay, but she rather thought that after living for so long by herself, she would like to have a ground floor flat somewhere of her own. Then she could have Fury back when he was well enough to leave the kennels.

'But what about all Belle's pretty things?' asked Claire.

'My friend went up there this morning to see that the workmen had nailed up the window the burglar got in by. She brought me back my most precious things, things I wouldn't want to be without. The rest will stay in the house,' said Miss Maine, 'and be part of the museum. I don't want them any more. It was foolish of me to hang on to them for so long. Let other people get pleasure out of them now.'

'Well,' said Aunty Pat, making a joke of it, 'I don't suppose Tomkin's ghost will climb the hill to look into the windows of the house once it's turned into a museum.'

'Oh, that old story,' said Miss Maine. 'Tomkin wasn't the only young man who lived in those cottages and long after he'd left for America, one of his friends used to creep up the alley. But it wasn't to see Belle. Oh dear, no! He was after one of the kitchenmaids. Ghosts, indeed!'

'Tomkin didn't drown himself, then?' asked Kate.

'No, of course not. He went to New York and made a fortune running a livery stable there. That's a place where you hire horses and carriages. After many years in America he came back with his American wife and sons, and settled down to become a pillar of the church and a town councillor. They've even got a street named after him somewhere. Drowned, indeed! Why, I heard the other day that one of his grandsons is standing for the local council elections. And I shall vote for him, too, when the time comes.'

When it was time to go, Miss Maine drew Kate to her and pressed a small book into her hands. 'This belonged to my father when he was a child. I'd like you to have it now. From an Old Soldier to a young one, eh?'

It was a very old book, much dog-eared. Claire would probably turn up her nose at it because it was so old and tatty, but Kate thought it was lovely. There was a picture of Jesus on the cover, holding out his arms to a child, who was running towards him. Kate just knew that the next minute the child would be swept up into Jesus' strong arms and feel safe.

'Thank you,' she said, and meant it.

'Well, Kate,' said her aunt as they drove home. 'It's nearly the end of your week's stay. I must say I shall feel quite sorry to part with you, and so will Claire.'

Kate wasn't sure about that. Claire hadn't actually lashed out at Kate that day, but she hadn't apologised for her previous bad behaviour and she wasn't making any great effort to be friends now.

Aunty Pat nudged Claire. 'You will be sorry to see Kate go, won't you?'

'Yes,' said Claire, but not as if she meant it. She turned to Kate and said politely, 'What would you like to do on your last day?'

Eloise winked at Kate over Claire's head. Kate grinned back. She knew what Eloise meant. Claire was making an effort even if it didn't come from the heart.

Kate said, 'Oh, we'll play at anything you like.'

'I suppose I could let you have a go on my computer.'

'Lovely,' said Kate, hiding her surprise.

Claire sighed and snuggled back against Eloise's side She wasn't being rude to Eloise any more. Perhaps Eloise would be able to get through to her in future.

A lot of good had come out of their little adventure. Claire had learned something and so had Kate. Kate didn't think she and Claire would ever be really good friends, but at least they'd got over hating one another.

Kate felt she'd grown up a lot since the half-term began.